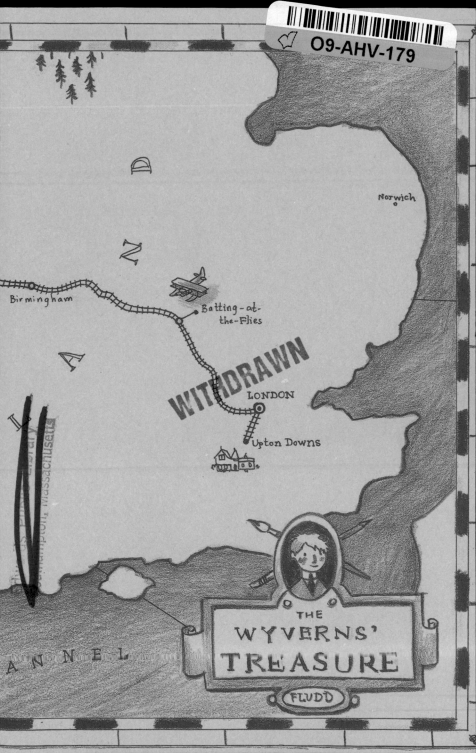

Nathaniel Fludd

Nathaniel Fludd
BEASTOLOGIST

BOOK THREE

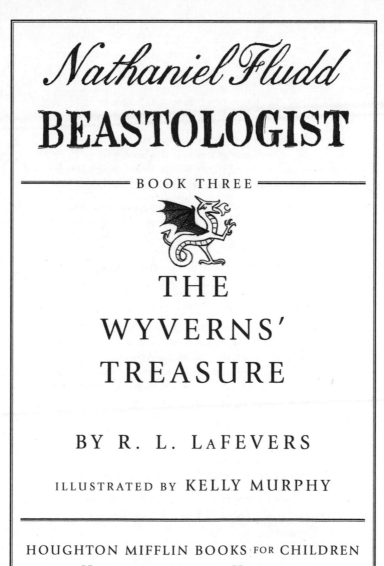

THE WYVERNS' TREASURE

BY R. L. LaFEVERS

ILLUSTRATED BY KELLY MURPHY

HOUGHTON MIFFLIN BOOKS FOR CHILDREN
Houghton Mifflin Harcourt
BOSTON   NEW YORK   2010

Houghton Mifflin Books for Children is an imprint of
Houghton Mifflin Harcourt Publishing Company.

www.hmhbooks.com

The text of this book is set in ITC Giovanni.
The illustrations are pen and ink.

Library of Congress Cataloging-in-Publication Data

La Fevers, R. L. (Robin L.)
The wyverns' treasure / by R.L. LaFevers ; illustrated by Kelly Murphy.
p. cm. — (Nathaniel Fludd, beastologist ; bk. 3)
Summary: When Nathaniel and Aunt Phil are summoned to the Welsh countryside
to calm the giant dragons known as wyverns, they suspect the problem was
caused by the same sinister man who has been trying to steal *The Book of Beasts*.
ISBN 978-0-547-31618-5
[1. Adventure and adventurers—Fiction. 2. Aunts—Fiction. 3. Dragons—Fiction.
4. Animals, Mythical—Fiction. 5. Orphans—Fiction. 6. Wales—Fiction.]
I. Murphy, Kelly, 1977–ill. II. Title.
PZ7.L1414Wyv 2010   [Fic]—dc22   2010006786

Manufactured in the United States of America
DOC 10 9 8 7 6 5 4 3 2 1
4500251923

Chapter One

THERE WERE TIMES when Nathaniel Fludd wasn't sure he'd survive living with Aunt Phil.

"Hold on!" she called over her shoulder. "The field's a bit bumpy."

Today was one of those times. With his feet resting on the weasels' crate, Nate gripped the sides of the cockpit. He had no idea if all pilots were this bad at landings or if it was just Aunt Phil.

The nose of the plane dipped down. They were coming

in a little fast, it seemed to Nate. And low, he thought, as they clipped a tree, shaving a good three feet off the top. Unable to stand it, he closed his eyes.

They landed with a jolt that sent his knees clacking into his chin. As they bounced and rolled to a stop, he tasted blood from where he'd bit his tongue. Once Aunt Phil cut the engine, Nate's pet gremlin, Greasle, popped her head out of his rucksack. "Is she done with all her hopping and bopping?"

"If you're wondering if we've landed, yes," Nate said.

Aunt Phil jumped out and came around to the side. "Can you hand me that crate?" she asked.

"Sure." Nate grasped the crate by the sides and hoisted it over the edge of the cockpit. Aunt Phil took it with a grunt. Then Nate grabbed his rucksack—Greasle and all—and climbed out of the plane. He felt like laughing for joy at the feel of solid ground under his feet.

Aunt Phil set the crate down on the grass and opened it. Roland and Sallie raced out, eager for their freedom after such a long journey. Nate watched as the weasels made a mad dash toward the nearby trees. "Will they come back, do you think?" he asked.

"Of course they will, in a day or two. This is their home, after all. And speaking of home," Aunt Phil said, "now that we're here, I'll have to do something about that gremlin of yours."

Hearing Aunt Phil's words, Greasle dived down into the depths of Nate's pack.

Aunt Phil did not like gremlins. She thought they were pests, and she hadn't been happy when Nate had rescued Greasle. But Greasle had become his best friend, and he couldn't imagine life without her. Even so, he kept his mouth closed. For now. Later, after Aunt Phil had had a decent meal and a hot bath, he'd try to talk her into letting him keep the gremlin.

Completely unaware of his scheming, Aunt Phil put her hands on her hips and looked toward the house. "I wonder where Cornelius is? He's usually here to welcome me home."

"Maybe he's sulking because we actually *made* it home. He was pretty certain I'd mess things up."

"Heard that, did you? I was afraid you had, but don't mind old Corny. He's gotten a bit protective from having lived through so many generations of Fludds." She grabbed the last pack. "Come on, let's get inside. I could do with a nice strong cup of tea."

Nate followed Aunt Phil to the back door, then nearly bumped into her as she stopped unexpectedly. "That's odd," she said.

"What's odd?"

"The back door is off its hinges." Scowling, she put her finger to her lips, then cautiously pushed the door open.

It took Nate a moment to realize what he was seeing. The house had never been tidy, but now it was in shambles. Tables were overturned and drawers were pulled out of bureaus. Some of the maps had been ripped from the wall and others were missing entirely. All the navigational instruments had been knocked from the shelves.

"Corny," Aunt Phil whispered. Then louder. "Cornelius!" It was hard to miss the note of panic in her voice. She ran into the kitchen. Cooking pots littered the floor and broken crockery was scattered everywhere. "Cornelius!" Aunt Phil called out again. "Are you here?"

They listened for a long moment, hearing nothing but echoing silence. Aunt Phil's shoulders drooped.

There was a faint rustling behind them. "Philomena? Is that really you?"

"Cornelius!" Aunt Phil whirled around. Her face lit up with relief as the dodo emerged from under the kitchen sink. "You're unharmed!"

"Harrumph," the dodo squawked. "If you call being browbeaten and terrorized *unharmed*, I suppose you could say that."

Indeed, the bird's feathers were all ruffled and askew.

"Poor Corny!" Aunt Phil knelt down in front of him. "Here, let me have a look at you."

It seemed to Nate that Cornelius was trying to look as pathetic as possible.

"I see the boy made it back alive," the dodo sniffed.

Nate wanted to shout, *Yes, I made it back, you dumb dodo!* Instead, he kicked at a tin can on the floor and said, "You've got a bit of rubbish stuck to your tail feathers."

Cornelius gave a small squawk of dismay. "Where?" he asked, craning his neck, trying to see his own backside.

Nate smiled in satisfaction, and Aunt Phil threw him a reproachful glance. "Nate did very well, Cornelius. I told you he would." Then she changed the subject. "Can you tell us what happened?" As she talked, her hands gently poked at Cornelius, looking for any serious damage.

"Two days ago a plane landed in the backyard. At first I thought it was you—you were late coming back, you know," he said accusingly.

"I know. We had a crisis in Africa. The basilisk escaped. Or was let loose. Your story first, then I will tell you ours."

"Just as I reached the back door to greet you, it flew open, knocked off its hinges. It caught me full on. I was lucky I wasn't killed."

"Indeed," Aunt Phil murmured comfortingly.

"The blow knocked me to the ground and stunned me. That worked to my advantage, actually. The intruder didn't notice me until later, and then he thought I was stuffed.

I'm quite sure that's what saved my life." The dodo paused, eliciting another dose of sympathy from Aunt Phil.

"Then the blackguard searched the house from top to bottom. Inside and out. He never gave a single thought as to what a mess he was making or what he was destroying, as you can see." Nate's rucksack rustled and he felt Greasle stick her head out so she could hear better.

"Was he alone?" Aunt Phil asked.

"Yes. After searching the entire house, he left. Empty-handed, I might add. Whatever he was searching for, he didn't find. I then dragged myself to the nearest hiding place and waited until it was safe to come out."

"For two whole days?" Nate asked.

The dodo fixed Nate with a baleful glare. "They say criminals always return to the scene of the crime. It seemed best to be on the safe—*what*," he asked, seeing Greasle for the first time, "is *that*?"

Aunt Phil waved his question aside. "A gremlin. I'll explain later. Did you get a look at the intruder?" Aunt Phil asked.

"I'll say. For three hours, as he ransacked the house, I had nothing to do *but* look at him. I hardly dared blink for fear he'd realize I wasn't stuffed." He sniffed again. "As if a beastologist would own a stuffed animal of any sort."

"Well, what did he look like?" Aunt Phil asked, a trace of impatience creeping into her voice.

Cornelius blinked his big yellow eyes at her. "Like you," he said.

Chapter Two

WHATEVER SHE'D BEEN EXPECTING, it wasn't this. Aunt Phil dropped back on her heels. "Are you sure?"

"How tall was he?" Nate interrupted.

"A bit shorter than Philomena," the dodo answered.

"And was he thin? Round?" Nate asked.

"Shaped a bit like a barrel," the dodo replied. "But why do you care? It's not as if you'd recognize another Fludd if you saw one."

Nate's cheeks grew warm at the scorn in Cornelius's voice. "It just so happens I saw a man exactly like that in

Arabia," Nate said hotly. "He was trying to steal *The Book of Beasts*. Greasle and I fought him off."

Cornelius ignored Nate's outburst and answered Aunt Phil's initial question. "Yes, I'm sure. He had the same ginger hair as you and the boy. Not to mention, I've been around enough Fludds to recognize their features when I see them."

Thoroughly confused, Nate turned to Aunt Phil. "But I thought you were my last remaining relative?"

Cornelius cast an accusing look at Aunt Phil. "Do you mean to tell me you've said nothing of Octavius Fludd to him?"

Aunt Phil waved his scolding aside. "We were rather busy, you know. And there were so many other important things to tell him. I didn't get around to mentioning it."

"Who is Octavius Fludd?" Nate asked.

"Do you remember me telling you that there was an eighth Fludd son? The family's black sheep?"

Nate nodded.

"Cornelius is suggesting that our mysterious intruder is one of his descendants. I believe his name is Obediah, but I'd have to consult our records to be sure. The information we have about that branch of the family is rather sketchy."

"But if he's related to you, why would he do this?" Nate surveyed the damage done to Aunt Phil's house.

"That would be where the black-sheep part comes in," Cornelius said dryly.

"I'm afraid it's a rather long story." Aunt Phil fetched the rubbish bin from under the sink and carried it over to the stove. She began tossing pieces of broken crockery into the trash. "Octavius was the son who got stuck with the northeastern exploration in Russia and Muscovy. It was a frozen, bitter wasteland, which turned him into a frozen, bitter man. Octavius soon stopped reporting his findings for the mapping project and withheld information on his explorations. Concerned, Sir Mungo sent one of his other sons, Henricus, to check on him. However, Octavius was convinced his own father and brothers were conspiring against him to banish him to that desolate place. He swore eternal vengeance, and Henricus barely made it back with his life."

"But that was hundreds of years ago," Nate said, tossing a smashed cake plate into the rubbish bin.

"Ah, but hatred feeds hatred. Octavius raised his sons to hate the rest of the Fludds, and his sons taught their own the same lesson. There was never any cooperation between the family branches. In fact, throughout the years they often worked against us, trying to beat us to new frontiers. Without intending to, we became caught up in a desperate competition. They would not share their information with us. They became wildly territorial and set upon any Fludd who ventured into their frozen wasteland—oh!"

"What?" Cornelius and Nate said at the exact same time. The dodo tossed Nate a quelling look.

"Well, as I told Nate, the man we ran into in Africa seemed to know with unerring accuracy the exact location of both the phoenix and the basilisk. This led me to think he had somehow acquired Sir Mungo Fludd's *Geographica* . . ."

"Which the boy's father had the only copy of," Cornelius added.

"Precisely. But it just now occurred to me, Nate's parents were exploring the frozen north. Is it possible that Obediah saw them as trespassing in his territory?"

"I'd think more than a possibility," Cornelius said. "It seems to me the bigger question is, did he arrange the deaths? Or merely claim *The Geographica* after they'd already been lost?"

Nate's entire body went hot, and then cold. "Are you saying you think they might have been killed on purpose?"

"That is what I intend to find out," Aunt Phil said. There was a moment of silence as they all considered what this might mean.

Deciding it was safe, Greasle crawled all the way out of Nate's backpack and onto his shoulder. "Seems to me this family spends too much time thinking about them book things. Doncha got any food around here?"

Cornelius turned a disbelieving gaze on Nate. "A gremlin? You actually picked a gremlin for a companion? No self-respecting beastologist would do that. They choose

elegant or exotic animals, like a dodo, say. Or a satyr. Wolfgang Fludd had one of those. And Gordon Fludd had a manticore."

"And I believe Leopold had a polar bear," Aunt Phil added thoughtfully.

"Yes, but never a pest," the dodo harrumphed.

"I'm no pest!" Stung to action, Greasle jumped off Nate's shoulder. Once on the floor, she hurried over to a teacup. "See? At least I gots fingers what can pick stuff up and be helpful-like." She wrinkled her nose at the dodo's wings, then reached out and grabbed the handle of the teacup. Next to her, it was nearly the size of a bathtub. She began dragging it to the rubbish bin, her face screwed up with the effort.

Nate bent down and plucked the cup from the ground, setting it on the counter.

"Ain't you going to put it in there, like she did?"

"Not this one," Nate said. Then he whispered out of the corner of his mouth. "It's not broken."

"Oh." Greasle's ears drooped. She looked from the cup to the broken pieces in the trash, trying to figure out the difference. Nate supposed it didn't make any sense if you'd never actually seen a teacup before.

"I have made up my mind," Aunt Phil announced.

Nate and Greasle turned their attention back to Aunt Phil. Had she decided about Greasle, then? Nate squared his shoulders and tried to come up with an argument as to why he should be able to keep the gremlin.

"Nate and I must go to London tomorrow and meet with his parents' lawyer," she continued. "Surely he'll have some more information he can share with us."

The thought of answers ignited a spark of hope in Nate and chased all thoughts of arguing from his head.

They had a quick dinner of tinned sardines on burned toast. After that, Aunt Phil called a neighbor and arranged for him to come over the next day and clean up the mess the intruder had left.

Nate was so tired he was stumbling when he finally

reached his bedroom on the second floor. Had he really once thought it rough and bare? After sleeping on the sand, in tents, and on the bumpy ground, this room was a luxury.

Greasle, however, wrinkled her nose. "It's so big," she said, huddling nearer. "So much empty space. I don't likes it," she said with a tiny shudder.

Nate figured if you were used to small, tight places, like engines, the room would seem very odd. "The bed is soft," he pointed out, trying to find something she might like.

But Greasle was looking at the window, her face bright. "It has snacks!" She scampered over and plucked a large dead fly from the sill, and popped it into her mouth.

Now it was Nate's turn to shudder. "Do you have to do that?"

"I tolds you I was hungry."

Nate sighed. "Come on, let's get ready for bed."

He needed to take a bath first. Greasle wanted to watch, so Nate had to explain that for humans, bathing was *private*. But after he'd scrubbed himself clean and put on an old nightshirt, he let Greasle into the bathroom.

As Nate brushed his teeth, Greasle studied the water curiously.

"You should probably take a bath, too," Nate said. "To wash all that oil and dirt off you."

"Nuh-unh," she said, recoiling. "Gremlins don't likes no nasty wet stuff."

"How do you know if you've never tried it?"

"How does you know you doesn't likes oil if you never eats it?" she asked.

Nate opened his mouth, then closed it, then finally said, "Because."

Greasle folded up her arms and looked smug. "Exactly."

Even though Nate was back in a comfortable bed, it took a while for him to fall asleep. His head was too full of possibilities. Ideas and unspoken hopes flitted around like moths, bumping into the one hope he dared not voice: Could his parents possibly still be alive?

Chapter Three

*E*ARLY THE NEXT MORNING, Aunt Phil shouldered her pack and led Nate and Greasle out to the motorbike in her garage. While Greasle had not been crazy about the bath or bedroom, she was delighted with the motorbike. She petted it fondly and even licked the exhaust pipe when she thought no one was looking.

Aunt Phil had Nate crawl into the funny little sidecar. Once he was settled, she started up the bike. As she drove them to the train station, Nate quickly realized that driving with her was almost as terrifying as flying.

If the motorbike made Greasle happy, the train waiting for them at the station made her ecstatic. "It's like a giant plane!" she said, clapping her hands in delight.

"Well, it doesn't fly, exactly," Nate tried to explain. "See? It has wheels."

"I don'ts cares about them. It's the engine I wants to see." She smacked her lips.

Aunt Phil frowned. "This is exactly the sort of thing I was worried about; gremlins could quickly infect all sorts of engines and motors. You should have left her at home."

Nate opened his eyes wide and tried to look innocent. "But then she'd be all alone with your plane. I didn't think you'd like that."

Aunt Phil grimaced. "No, I wouldn't have liked that. But keep a close eye on her. And I *will* deal with this when we return."

Nate and Greasle exchanged worried looks, and then Nate scooped her up. "Be good," he said, putting her back into his rucksack. Once he'd fastened the top, he could hardly even hear her squeaks of protest.

As Nate settled into his seat, he realized this train ride wasn't nearly as nerve-racking as the last one he'd taken. He wasn't alone, for one thing. But also, compared to the past two weeks, a train ride to the city was a piece of cake. He spent the whole time drawing.

They arrived in London just before lunch. When they got on board a double-decker bus, Greasle wanted to know if it had two engines.

"No," Aunt Phil said. "And get back into the pack before anyone sees you." She let Nate sit up on the top level, something his old governess, Miss Lumpton, had never let him do.

When the bus reached their stop, Aunt Phil checked her slip of paper for directions. "It should be just down this street here," she said, pointing the way.

"It *looks* familiar," Nate said.

"Excellent. Come along."

They proceeded down the street until they came to number 436. Nate scratched his head, puzzled. "It didn't have boards on the windows last time I was here."

Aunt Phil pursed her lips. "Well, it looks quite deserted

now." All the windows were boarded shut, and there was a great thick lock on the door. Aunt Phil knocked anyway, but there was no answer. Nate sat down on the top step and rested his chin on his knees.

"That's a bit of a setback." Aunt Phil took a seat beside him.

"So now what?" Nate asked. His voice wobbled, so he cleared his throat.

"Now we try to track down Miss Lumpton. Do you know where she lived before she came to take care of you?"

Nate shook his head. "I never thought about her living someplace else. She's been with me since I can remember."

"Well, she must have a home or some remaining family. Perhaps there is a record of it back at your parents' house. At the very least, I'd like to search there to see if there was any correspondence with your parents."

"I told you, they never sent any letters," Nate said glumly.

"That you know of," Aunt Phil clarified. "Come along. If we hurry to the station, we can catch a train and be at your house by teatime."

Chapter Four

THEY ARRIVED IN UPTON DOWNS just after lunch. Stepping off the train, Nate was flooded with sights and sounds that were achingly familiar. And welcome. He wondered if he would see anybody he knew. Then he realized he didn't actually *know* that many people. Just Miss Lumpton, the grocer, their gardener, and the milkman, who had come to their house Mondays and Thursdays.

Upton Downs was too small to have buses or taxicabs, but the stationmaster recognized Nate and let them use his bicycle.

"But there's only one," Nate said, plucking his gremlin away from the greasy chain.

"It will do. Hop on." Aunt Phil patted the handlebars.

"There?"

"Of course. We used to do it all the time as children. Now come along. I'll give you a boost."

With Nate perched precariously on the handlebars, Aunt Phil began pedaling down the street. The bike wobbled horribly, and Nate held on for dear life. Every time they went over a bump in the road, his teeth snapped together. As they came around the last bend, the familiar tower roof of Nate's house came into view. His heart lifted and he forgot all about the handlebars digging into his backside. He was almost home. Had it really been only two weeks? It felt more like two years.

When they turned into the driveway, Nate was shocked at how overgrown the lawn was. Normally cut short, it was now up to his knees. Even worse was the deserted feel the house had. All the gabled windows stared back at him like empty eyes; an air of loneliness and neglect hung over the house like a cloud. As Nate got off the bike, he tried to swallow a huge lump of disappointment.

They hadn't gone far when Aunt Phil put her hand on his shoulder and stopped him.

"What?" he asked.

"The door is ajar. Look."

Indeed, the dark green door stood open a few inches. Was someone home after all? Excited, Nate hurried forward. "Miss Lumpton! Miss Lumpton, I'm back!" He clattered into the hallway, his feet halting at the great emptiness there.

"She's not here, Nate," Aunt Phil said from behind him. "In fact, I think your house has been ransacked, just like mine."

Aunt Phil was right. In the living room, the green velvet sofa that hardly anyone ever sat on had been sliced to ribbons. Fluffy white stuffing spilled out onto the floor. Tables had been swept clear, lamps overturned. The kitchen reeked of sour milk.

"Pew!" said Greasle, pinching her nose shut.

"Let's try upstairs," Aunt Phil said, without much hope.

Nate led her up the stairs. She stopped at the first room on the right. "Whose room is this?" she asked.

"Miss Lumpton's."

"Excellent. Just what I was looking for." She came around him into the room, then frowned. "Where are all her things?"

Nate shrugged. "I don't know."

"Did she take them with her that day you went to London together?"

Nate thought back to the few possessions in the suitcase of hers he'd grabbed by mistake. "No, she packed enough only for a night or two."

"Which means she must have returned at some point to collect the rest of her belongings. Hmmm." Aunt Phil did a quick inspection of the room but found nothing remotely interesting. She even looked in the little wastebasket near the bed. She fished a piece of paper out and slipped it into her pocket.

"What did you find?" Nate asked.

"Not much," she admitted. "Was there a study or library she used?"

"We both shared the library downstairs. I'll show you." He turned and hurried down the stairs, glad to be away from the empty bedrooms. "Here." He opened the door to

the library, where he'd done his lessons under Miss Lumpton's watchful eye.

This room, too, had been searched. All the papers and books on the desks and tables had been swept to the floor. The towering bookcases were knocked over, their entire contents spilled out onto the rug. "Well, this makes no sense," Aunt Phil said. "If Obediah Fludd had *The Geographica*, why would he search your parents' house?"

Nate nudged a globe with his foot and watched it roll across the floor. "Maybe he doesn't have it."

"But then how was he able to pinpoint the beasts' locations so accurately?"

"You did say there were other bestiaries."

"Yes, but they are far less reliable. Hang on a minute. I want to have a quick look in the desk." She went over to the large mahogany desk, righted the chair behind it, and sat down. Quickly and efficiently she opened the drawers and began rifling through them.

"Wow, this is some mess, it is," Greasle said.

"Yeah," Nate agreed. It was hard to believe he was staring at *his* home, *his* house. He could not get his mind around the fact that someone had thought there was something that valuable here.

"Well," Aunt Phil said with a sigh. "There's nothing. No journals, no letters, nothing. I cannot believe your parents wouldn't have sent some record of their journeys and discoveries over the years. It's part of the Fludd Protocol—always be sure a record of your discoveries is left behind, in case . . ." Her voice trailed off and she cleared her throat, as if remembering Nate was in the room. "We'll just have to move to plan B," she said, firmly shutting the last desk drawer.

"What's plan B?" Nate asked.

"I'm not sure yet. I need to think on it a bit."

Nate left Aunt Phil sitting at the old desk and wandered into the hall and out the front door. Greasle scampered off to chase a dragonfly buzzing among the overgrown grass. Nate sat on the front porch, his shoulders sagging. There were no answers, no new clues. Feeling hopeful and then having it taken away was even worse than having no hope at all, he decided.

There was a loud squawk. Then a faint *thud*. He sat up, suddenly alert. Greasle was nowhere to be seen. However, the overgrown grass off to his right was waving crazily. He got to his feet and took a step toward the wriggling grass. "Greasle?" he called out, feeling nervous.

"I caughts something," she squeaked. "And it's a biggie."

Chapter Five

AUNT PHIL APPEARED on the front step. "Nate, where is your father's—what's your gremlin got now?" she asked.

"I don't know." Nate hurried off into the grass. Greasle had a bird in a chokehold and was trying valiantly to drag it out into the open. It was almost as big as she was and was flapping its wings madly.

"It's a pigeon," Nate called out to Aunt Phil. "Or maybe a dove. I can't tell."

"Hold still, you big bag of feathers," Greasle muttered. She dug in her heels and tugged.

"Stop!" Aunt Phil called out. Nate and Greasle froze. "Planes, trains, and motorcars aren't enough for you? Now you're going to eat my messenger as well?"

Nate and Greasle looked at her blankly.

"That's a carrier pigeon. With a message. See?" She pointed to the small pouch strapped to one of its feet. "Let it go," Aunt Phil ordered.

Greasle scowled. "I caughts it fair and square."

"*Now,*" Aunt Phil said in her most stern voice.

"It's just going to fly away again," Greasle mumbled. With one last glare at Aunt Phil, she let go of her prize.

With a disgruntled coo, the bird rose into the air and headed straight for Aunt Phil. It landed on her shoulder and turned a fierce, beady eye on the gremlin.

As Aunt Phil took the small pouch from its leg, Nate asked Greasle, "Do you really eat pigeons?"

The gremlin shrugged. "I don'ts know. I eats anything if I'm hungry enough."

"This is a prime example of why we don't need a gremlin wandering around," Aunt Phil pointed out before reading the note. "It's from Cornelius," she said at last. "He's received word from our caretaker in Wales. The wyverns are on the rampage for some reason and he needs immediate assistance."

"Can't somebody else go?" Nate asked. "We're kind of busy here trying to find some clues."

Aunt Phil looked at him over the top of the note. "Do you have any idea what damage a rampaging wyvern can cause?"

"How could I?" Nate asked, exasperated. "I don't even know what a wyvern *is*."

"Oh. Right. Well, it's a dragon—one of the last surviving breeds of dragon in western Europe. All those horrid dragon deeds you've read about in stories have been done by rampaging wyverns: breathing fire, ruining crops, drying up rivers, stealing cattle and sheep and young children. If the wyverns are on the rampage, it's our job to stop them. It's part of being a beastologist. Besides," Aunt Phil said gently, "there's nothing more to learn here."

"You mean we're going to leave without any answers?"

"What else would you have me do?"

Nate didn't know, but he was sure it wasn't *leave*. "But what about my parents?"

"We've come to a bit of a dead end," Aunt Phil said. "And

we can't let other people come to harm in the meantime. There is no one else, Nate," she reminded him. "Only us. Now come along. We can talk more on the way. We must get there before they do any real damage."

Something big and hot and prickly rose up in Nate's chest, but he tamped it back down. He gave a nearby pebble a violent kick before following Aunt Phil to the bicycle.

Back at the Upton Downs train station, Aunt Phil used the stationmaster's telephone to put a call through to the caretaker. She told him they would take the train directly to Beddgelert, and he promised to be there to meet them.

"We're not even going to go home first?" Nate asked.

"No time," she said as the train pulled into the station. They bustled aboard and settled into their seats. Nate looked out the window, wondering if this would be the last time he ever saw his little village. The whistle blew and the train chugged forward until Upton Downs was merely a smudge in the distance.

Once under way, Aunt Phil pulled *The Book of Beasts* from the large pack she carried with her at all times. She opened the book to *W* and quickly found *Wyvern*. Nate scooted closer and peered at the picture. He'd never seen a dragon before.

The beast seemed impossibly big. In the picture, it towered over the oxen it had just snagged with its enormous, sharp talons. Its long body was serpentine and covered in scales. Immense wings sprouted from its shoulders. The tail was very nearly as long as its body and ended in a sharp point. The idea of meeting one of those face-to-face made Nate's insides turn all watery.

He checked to see if Aunt Phil was watching, then opened the top of his rucksack so Greasle could see, too. The gremlin crawled out, her eyes growing wide when she saw the picture. In a quiet voice, Nate began to read.

Wyverns are one of the last remaining dragons in the west, confined mostly to their nesting area in the mountains of Snowdonia, Wales. From the tip of their snout to the barb at the end of their serpentine tail, they can reach a length of thirty feet. They stand approximately twenty feet high and have two legs and a pair of magnificent wings. Each of the wing spines has a large talon attached to it.

They are quite fond of sheep, cattle, and oxen but will settle for humans if no hooved animals can be found. They will also feed on trout and salmon, but consider those more of a supplement than a true meal. They mate for life and hatch their eggs in an underground cavern. The hatchlings remain there until their scales have fully hardened and they can brave the outside world. Safe

W

Wyvern

30 feet

in the caves, the dragonlings practice hunting, hoarding, and breathing small plumes of fire. All the adult dragons share in the parenting duties.

It takes five years for wyverns to reach maturity. They spend the last year of childhood hunting side by side with the adults.

The wyverns' method of attack involves swooping down from the sky amid loud shrieks that are intended to paralyze their victims with fear. They use the massive talons on their feet for grabbing prey and the smaller claws on their wings to hold the prey while they rip into it with their razor-sharp teeth. The wyverns' lashing barbed tail can also do great damage.

Since the wyverns entered into the Covenant with Lludd, the attacks on humans have been few and far between, usually perpetrated by a rogue wyvern who has been banned from his herd or a young wyvern who hasn't fully learned the rules yet.

Well, that last part was almost reassuring, Nate thought. "Who is this Lludd fellow?" he asked Aunt Phil.

She looked up from the book. "He was an earlier ancestor of Sir Mungo's. A Welsh chieftain, to be exact." She paused, thinking. "I suppose, in a way, he was the first beastologist, even though he lived long before Honorius coined the term. If it hadn't been for him, wyverns would still be attacking people and doing great damage and destruction. Would you like to hear the story?"

"Yes, please." Nate settled more comfortably into his seat. It had been a long time since anyone had told him a story.

"Well over a thousand years ago," Aunt Phil began, "a few hundred years before Sir Mungo Fludd was born, Lludd ruled over northern Wales. He was a wise ruler and his people trusted him. However, back then Wales was plagued with wyverns."

Nate shuddered and tried to imagine living in a place where dragons roamed free.

"The wyverns fought among themselves, snatched sheep and oxen from the fields, and terrorized the people with their fire-breathing skills. It was quite a problem, so Lludd decided to do something about it. Luckily, he had a brother who was even wiser than he was. This brother told Lludd to dig an enormous pit on the hill known as Dinas Emrys. When the pit was big enough, he was to fill it with mead, then lay a cloth over it to hide it.

"Attracted by the smell of mead, the wyverns flocked

to Dinas Emrys. They didn't see the pit hidden under the cloth, so they landed on top of it, and fell into the hole and were trapped. Lludd refused to let them out until they all agreed to a series of conditions, which we know as the Covenant."

"What kind of conditions?" Nate asked.

"They agreed to keep their fire breathing confined to specific areas where it wouldn't do any harm and to stop treating the villagers' herds of oxen and sheep as a pantry. In return, we promised to leave their caverns alone and quit trying to find their treasure. We also promised to provide them with livestock they could eat." Aunt Phil was silent for a moment before continuing. "Luckily, they were a bit tipsy from the mead or they might never have agreed."

Chapter Six

*N*ATE VAGUELY REMEMBERED being awakened during the night and changing trains three times. Now he sat, trying to blink the sleep from his eyes and feeling rumpled as the train chugged into the station.

"Ah, we're awake now," Aunt Phil said, closing her book.

Doesn't she ever sleep? Nate wondered.

"We've just arrived in Beddgelert," she told him. "And there's Dewey now, come to pick us up." She pointed to a gentleman waiting on the platform. He held his tweed cap in his hand and was crooked over a bit, as if he'd spent his whole life ducking. He had a thick white mustache that looked like the handlebars of a bicycle.

"It would probably be best if you put your gremlin away until we clear the station." Aunt Phil nodded at Greasle, who was curled up on top of Nate's sketchbook, fast asleep in his lap. "There's an awful lot of temptation out there."

Nate shook Greasle gently.

"I's awake," she murmured with a sigh. "And hungry. Is there anything to eat on this caboose?"

At the reminder of food, Nate's stomach growled, and he looked at Aunt Phil hopefully.

"We'll eat as soon as we get to Dewey's."

Nate held his pack open, and Greasle climbed in. "I's could starve by then," she grumbled before he managed to fasten down the lid.

As they got off the train, Dewey's face brightened at the sight of them. He glanced curiously at Nate, then bobbed his head at Aunt Phil. "Good to see ye, Dr. Fludd, and your young assistant." He winked at Nate, and Nate smiled back.

"Me car's this way, and I'll tell you of the problem while we drive, if'n you don't mind."

He herded them to the car, which turned out to be an ancient truck that coughed and spit when he started it. At the sound of the engine turning over, Greasle stuck her head out of the pack, startling Dewey. "Eh, what new beastie is this, then?" he asked.

"Since you've not been around planes much, you probably haven't met a gremlin before," Aunt Phil said. "Meet Greasle, Nate's temporary pet."

Dewey doffed his cap to the gremlin, which made her chortle with glee. She laughed so hard she tumbled off Nate's lap and he had to retrieve her from the floor.

"And this is my nephew, Nate, the next beastologist after me."

This time, not only did Dewey doff his cap, but he bowed his head slightly, which embarrassed Nate greatly. "Pleased to meet ye."

"So what's the situation?" Aunt Phil asked crisply.

"Well, the wyverns have been in a mighty uproar since just after feeding time yesterday morning. I thought it would die down, but it didn't, so I contacted you. They've been fetching and screaming, roaring and blowing plumes of smoke. Can't rightly figure out what's got them so riled up."

"That's not good."

"Aye. I managed to calm them down a bit with the news that you were on your way. They're waiting to parley with you right now. We'll head directly there, if'n you don't mind. Angry wyverns don't have much in the way of patience."

"Very well," Aunt Phil said, her words echoing in Nate's empty stomach. Almost as if reading his mind, Dewey looked down at him and winked. "And my Winifred sent a basket, as she knows the good doctor never takes the time to eat properly."

"And it is very much appreciated," Aunt Phil said. She fetched the basket from the floor of the truck and lifted the brightly checked cloth on top. Delicious smells floated upward and Nate's stomach growled again. She handed him a small meat pie shaped like a turnover. Nate was so hungry he didn't even ask what was in it. For once, he didn't care. He broke it in two and gave one half to Greasle.

Aunt Phil raised an eyebrow but didn't scold him. Instead, she silently handed him a second meat pie.

As they ate their lunch, the old truck rumbled and coughed its way through green hills scattered with harsh

gray rock. The farther away from the station they got, the rougher the terrain became. Soon the green slopes turned to jagged cliffs and crags. Overhead, clouds clustered around the tops of the mountains, darkening the sky until it was nearly purple. Nate thought he saw dark shapes darting behind the clouds, but he couldn't be sure. There was a brief flash of light that could have been a lightning bolt or a billow of fire.

The truck stopped and Dewey shut off the engine. "We've got to go on foot from here on up."

"That's me signal," Greasle said, and scrambled back into Nate's rucksack.

"Did you bring the necessities?" Aunt Phil asked Dewey as she got out of the truck.

"Yep, all right here." He patted the truck bed, where Nate saw an old leather satchel, a large barrel, and a wheelbarrow. As Aunt Phil reached for the satchel, Dewey set himself to removing the wheelbarrow and the barrel.

Aunt Phil set the satchel on the ground and opened it. "So Nate, your first lesson on wyverns. They can speak, but because of their immense size, the sound waves they produce are deeper and lower than humans can hear. They just sound like grumbles and mumbles to our naked ear. Therefore, we use these." From the pack, she produced a pair of crooked brass horns. She lifted one to her ear. "These special ear trumpets force the sound waves of the wyverns' voices to contract and shrink, making the words recognizable. Here. Hang it from your belt for easy access."

Nate took the horn from her and snapped the clip to his belt. He wrinkled his nose, then sniffed. "I smell smoke," he said.

"Nah, that's just the wyverns." Dewey hoisted the barrel from the truck bed and put it into the wheelbarrow. "I warned you they were impatient. The longer they wait, the madder they get."

"And the madder they are, the more smoke you'll smell," Aunt Phil explained. "That's the second lesson. In fact, if the smell of smoke and ash grows too strong, hit the ground, because they're about to blow."

Nate swallowed, trying to reassure himself that if Dewey and Aunt Phil weren't afraid to meet with angry wyverns, he shouldn't be either.

Dewey gripped the wheelbarrow handles and began steering the lumbering contraption toward the path.

"What's that for?" Nate skipped to catch up.

"It's the traditional peace offering for wyverns. A token to show them we mean no harm," Aunt Phil explained.

"Mead," Dewey added. "They're right fond of it. Have been ever since ol' Lludd gave 'em their first taste."

The smell of smoke and ash grew stronger the closer they got to the top of the hill. Nate also heard a rumbling sound, as if there were a thunderstorm lurking up above.

As they drew close to the ridge, Aunt Phil gave him a few last-minute instructions. "Don't look them in the eye until you've been introduced. They'll take that as a grave insult. Keep any shiny things in your pockets and don't take them out, or they'll think you've brought them a gift. Then you'll be stuck having to give it to them. Got it?"

Repeating the instructions to himself, Nate nodded. Before he had time to do more than that, they cleared the last switchback. He found himself atop a large hill encircled by stones. In the middle were three dragons—*wyverns*, he corrected. Remembering Aunt Phil's words, he jerked his gaze down before he could give offense. Even so, his quick glimpse had shown beasts so vast and terrible looking that he wanted to turn and run all the way back down the hill. Except his legs were shaking so badly, he didn't think he'd make it.

Chapter Seven

Out of the corner of his eye, Nate saw Aunt Phil bow. "Greetings, Urien," she said, then put the trumpet to her ear. Remembering, Nate scrambled to get his in place, too.

The wyvern spread his leathery wings wide—they were huge!—and roared. The great bellow of sound hurt Nate's ears. Safe in the rucksack, he felt Greasle tremble.

"Now, now, it's not as bad as all that," Aunt Phil said soothingly.

"The Covenant isss broken." The sound of the dragon's

voice was terrible, like the crackling of flames and the rumble of thunder, all at the same time.

"I got here as soon as I could."

The wyvern growled in response. The earth shook as he took a step closer, then another. Every bone in Nate's body shook in fear. He kept his eyes glued to the ground and prayed Aunt Phil knew what she was doing.

Something long and thin flickered in his direction, gracefully fluttering around his head. Nate peered up through his eyelashes to see what it was. The dragon's tongue.

"We sssmell a stranger. Did you bring a tasty morsel to appease usss?"

"Of course not," Aunt Phil snapped at the wyvern.

Beside him, Dewey made a strange choking sound. It took a moment before Nate recognized it was laughter.

"Don't worry. Just a little dragon humor," Aunt Phil explained. She turned back to the wyvern. "He's my nephew. He'll be the next beastologist after I'm gone, so you better treat him well." Out of the side of her mouth, she whispered to Nate, "Bow."

He bowed so low, his forehead practically touched the scorched ground beneath his feet.

"Greetingsss, youngling," the wyvern—Urien—said.

"You can stand up now and look at him," Aunt Phil instructed.

Slowly, Nate raised his eyes.

The wyvern was covered in gray and green scales that had a pearly sheen to them. Sharp teeth poked out from between his lips, and another row of toothy-looking spikes encircled his head. Two larger horns sat just over surprisingly delicate-looking ears. But what startled Nate the most were the eyes. Even though they were a roiling, boiling orange and red, they were filled with intelligence. There was also a glimmer of amusement, which made Nate relax, just the littlest bit. "Pleased to meet you," Nate said.

"He's sssmall," the wyvern said.

"Yes, but he'll grow soon enough. And we did bring you a gift," Aunt Phil said. "Here."

With a grunt, Dewey rolled the barrel of mead forward. "Here you go. A nice drop o' mead for you."

And a drop was all it would be for the dragon, Nate realized.

Urien bowed his head, rather regally, Nate thought, then motioned for one of the other wyverns to take it. The other dragon swooped forward and plucked it elegantly from the ground using the wicked-looking claw along the tip of his wing.

"Now," Aunt Phil said. "About this Covenant. How has it been broken? Did we not give you enough sheep? Do you need more oxen?"

"Intruder. Nasssty intruder sneaking around."

Aunt Phil glanced quickly at Nate, whose heart began to beat very, very fast. Could that mean . . . ?

"Have you seen any signs of a trespasser?" she asked Dewey.

He shrugged. "Not hide nor hair of anyone."

"Where?" Aunt Phil turned back to Urien. "Where did you see him?"

"Sssmelled him."

"Can you tell where the intruder is now?"

"Caves. Sssneaking around in our caves. You broke the agreement," the wyvern said. "We will punish."

"Now, now. The Covenant also clearly states that we have three days to make things right before you go on a rampage."

"Ssstranger arrived the night before last."

58

"Then that gives us a little over twenty-four hours to take care of the matter ourselves. By nightfall tomorrow. Do you agree?"

Urien sighed and Nate thought he sounded regretful, as if he were very much looking forward to a rampage. For the first time, Nate realized how hard it must be *not* to be able to do dragonish things when one was a dragon.

"As you wish."

"Excellent. We'll report back here then."

"Until then." The wyvern spread his giant wings, nearly

blocking out the sun, then launched into the air. Nate gasped as the powerful surge lifted the creature off his feet and set a small tornado of leaves and dust swirling in its wake. The other two followed, one grasping the tiny barrel in his claws. They were unexpectedly graceful in the air, he thought.

"Come along now," Aunt Phil said. "We haven't got much time to get to the bottom of this."

Chapter Eight

DEWEY LIVED IN THE STRANGEST HOUSE Nate had ever seen. It was built into the ground—a barrow, Aunt Phil called it. "All the caretakers have lived here since the very beginning. It took a while for the Covenant to stick, you see. There were lots of . . . *incidents,* until the wyverns managed to bring all their members into line. A house like this, with sod for a roof, was relatively flameproof."

Nate also met Dewey's wife, Winifred, who reminded him of a hen as she clucked around, making sure they had enough to eat and were comfortable.

She was quite taken with the gremlin. "What a charming wee doll you have there," she told Nate.

Embarrassed, he started to explain but was interrupted by Greasle herself. "I ain't no doll," she said, putting her hands on her hips. "I's a gremlin."

"Ah, and so I see," Winifred said. "And what exactly is a gremlin, then?"

Greasle opened her mouth, then closed it and looked at Nate. Nate shrugged. Was Greasle a person? An animal? He had no idea what a gremlin *was*. Except a pest occasionally,

according to Aunt Phil. He was guessing that wasn't the answer Greasle was looking for.

"A gremlin's me," Greasle finally said.

"Ah," Winifred said, as if that made perfect sense. "Good to know, then."

When she left the room, Greasle turned to Nate. "What's a doll?"

"A toy. Shaped like a tiny person."

"Maybe I is a doll, then."

"Nope. For one, you're alive. And two, you're not very humanlike."

After much argument, it was finally decided that Nate and Aunt Phil would spend the night, then set out first thing in the morning. Aunt Phil wanted to get moving immediately, but Dewey and Winifred convinced her a night's rest was in order.

When Dewey went to fetch their equipment, Nate and Aunt Phil were finally alone for a moment. The question that had been trying to burst out of Nate for the past hour wiggled free. "Do you think the intruder is Obediah Fludd?" he asked. Even though Obediah sounded like a despicable person, Nate thought he might be able to give them a clue about Nate's parents.

Aunt Phil paused in sorting through her gear. "I have to think so, Nate. It's too much of a coincidence that an entirely separate intruder has shown up here."

"Why is he visiting all the beasts? Do you think he wants to be a beastologist?"

"I don't think so. But that's one of my concerns. I can't imagine *what* he might be up to, which makes me very nervous."

"In stories, dragons have treasure, and you mentioned the wyverns' treasure. Maybe he's after that?"

"That would have been my first guess, except it doesn't explain what he wanted with the phoenix and the basilisk. No, I'm afraid he has something more sinister in mind."

"Like what?"

"Exploitation," she said, a look of disgust on her face.

Nate looked at her blankly.

"One of the reasons we beastologists take our job so seriously is for the beasts' protection. Ever since man learned of them, they have been hunted, trapped, snared, and captured. Often for a bit of claw or a tooth, a scale or two, a feather. That is why there are so very few left. It's hard to believe, but some of these beasts used to be so plentiful that they were considered pests. But now you and I must do everything in our power to help them survive."

"So what did he want with the basilisk?" Nate asked.

Aunt Phil shook her head. "Again, I haven't a clue."

"Do you think he meant to capture it?"

Aunt Phil pursed her lips thoughtfully. "That had occurred to me, but to what end?"

Nate shrugged. "It seems to me, if you had something like a basilisk, you could pretty much get anyone to do what you wanted because everyone would be so scared of it."

Aunt Phil looked at Nate as if he'd sprouted horns. "But of course! How clever of you, Nate! He could use it as a weapon or as a means of forcing all sorts of things."

Nate stood a little taller and tried to look clever rather than simply nervous. Heartened by Aunt Phil's praise, he asked the question that had haunted him since Urien had first spoken of the intruder. "Do you think Obediah will know where my parents are?"

Aunt Phil's face softened. "Oh, Nate, I'm sorry. I didn't mean to give you false hope. Just because I suspect Obediah may have obtained *The Geographica* doesn't mean I think your parents are still alive. It only means I think Obediah might have taken advantage of their death."

Nate's heart plummeted all the way to his toes. "But I thought you said . . ."

"I said I thought their disappearance was related to this stranger's sudden knowledge of where to find the beasts. Not the same thing at all, Nate. I'm sorry."

Nate reviewed their past conversations in his head. Aunt Phil was right. She'd never said they might still be alive. "Oh." He felt foolish and silly and, most of all, as if he was going to cry. He turned away before she could see. "Did you get everything you need out of your pack?" he asked.

"Yes, thank you. I've put everything I need in Dewey's flameproof one." Her voice was gentle, which made it even worse. Nate picked up her pack and lugged it to a corner of the room to give himself a moment of privacy.

Just then, Dewey returned carrying an enormous wad of gear in his arms. With a *thunk*, he set it down onto the table, then stood up and rubbed his back. "There you go, ma'am. I think that's everything."

"Excellent, Dewey!" Aunt Phil stood beside the table and began dividing it up. She handed Nate two coils of rope, some metal spikes that looked like giant nails, and a small pick. Last she gave him an enormous helmet. "What's that on top?" he asked, taking it from her.

"Ah, that was Dewey's brilliant idea."

The old man beamed.

"He figured out a way to bolt an electric lantern to the top. That way we can keep our hands free but still see where we're going in the caves."

Caves. Nate swallowed. Why did there always have to be caves?

Aunt Phil showed him how to fasten all his gear to his pack. When she was done, she placed *The Book of Beasts* on the table. "Come look at this so you can get an idea of the caverns' layout," she said.

Nate came over as she opened the book to the page on wyverns. The page after it was blank. Or so Nate thought. As he watched, Aunt Phil unfolded what turned out to be a map. "These are the caverns of Dinas Emrys, mapped by Llewellyn Fludd nearly four centuries ago."

Nate peered down at the page. The paper was old and thick, the writing very fancy and hard to read. The map itself looked like a maze, with paths that twisted and turned and ran into dead ends. It didn't look to Nate as though any of the tunnels led anywhere.

After studying the map for a few moments, Aunt Phil gave a brisk nod. "Exactly as I remember. Excellent." She folded it back up, shut the book, then stored it in her pack. "Oh, and one more thing. You'll need these." She dug into her pocket and put a handful of pennies into Nate's hand.

"What are these for?" he asked, staring at the shiny new coins in his palm.

"Some of these wyverns are young, Nate. They don't understand yet about covenants or parleys or any of that sort of thing. They are ruled by their base instincts: food, physical prowess, and treasure. They will see us and think *Food!* If that happens, the most effective way to get free will be to distract them with another of their base instincts— the desire for treasure. To wyverns, treasure simply means anything shiny. A new copper penny will be as exciting to them as gold sovereigns."

N

grand
cavern

hatcheries

chamber 4

n -

four-
alls

chamber 3

chamber 2

chamber 1

the f
Din

to Beddgelert

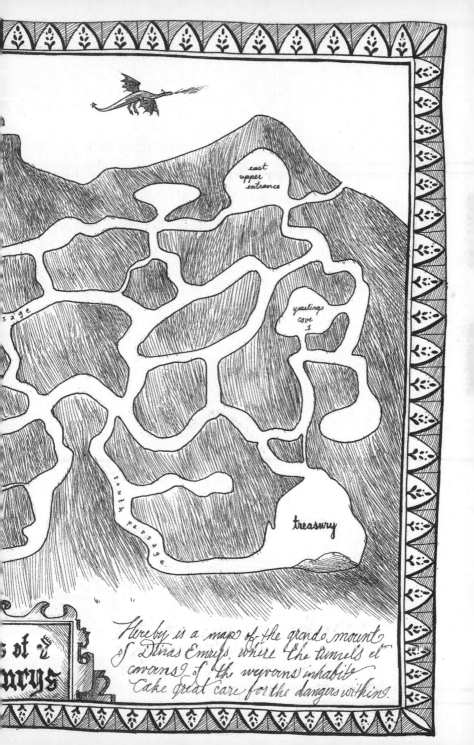

east
upper
entrance

yearlings
cave
1

passage

south passage

treasury

Hereby is a map of the grande mount of Dinas Emrys, where the tunnels et caverns of the wyverns inhabit. Take great care for the dangers within.

...s of
...nrys

"Won't the adults honor the Covenant and protect us?" Nate asked.

"The adults don't live in the caverns with their young. Most are too big to fit comfortably. I'm afraid we'll be on our own."

Nate spent the rest of the evening sketching and trying hard not to think of wyverns or bats or his parents.

Chapter Nine

WHEN THEY SET OUT EARLY the next morning, Dewey led them around to the back side of Dinas Emrys. At the base of the mountain, a thick iron gate blocked the opening to the cave. Dewey removed a large key and opened the lock. The gate screeched as he opened it.

"Do the wyverns try to get out often?" Nate asked.

"It's not to keep the beasties in, me boy." Dewey winked. "But to keep others out."

"Such as our intruder," Aunt Phil said, studying the ground near her feet.

Puzzled, Nate tried to see what she was doing. "What are you looking at?"

"This." Aunt Phil pointed to a footprint in the dirt. "Dewey, let me see the bottom of your boot."

The old gamekeeper scratched his head, then lifted his boot. Aunt Phil inspected the tread on the sole, then looked back at the footprint on the ground. "This is not yours. Take a look."

Dewey squinted down at it. "You're right about that. Plus them feet are quite a bit wider than mine."

"Perhaps just the right size for a round, barrel-shaped man," Aunt Phil muttered. "I have my key, Dewey, so you don't need to wait around for us. If we're not back three hours before the deadline, put out the warning and clear the hills. Be sure people know this is not a drill. They're to leave their herds and possessions and get out before the wyverns cut loose."

"I got the impression the beasts were quite looking forward to it," Dewey said.

"I did, too. All the more reason to get the villagers to safety without delay."

Dewey doffed his cap. "Aye, aye, doctor. And I'll be back in a wink to feed the young'uns. Just to keep 'em busy while you search the caves."

"That won't be necessary," Aunt Phil said.

"It won't hurt, neither," Dewey replied.

The gate clanged shut behind them and Nate heard the loud click as Dewey locked it. There was nowhere to go now but into the wyverns' cave.

Nate's breath began to come in fast, sharp gasps as he looked up toward the cavern ceiling, ready to duck.

"Don't worry, there aren't any bats here. There's too much light," Aunt Phil told him.

Nate stood up a little straighter. He knew it was silly to be afraid of bats when there were wyverns around, but he didn't seem to have any control over it.

The cavern itself wasn't very big. It went for a little ways, then dropped off to a large, shadowed pit below. A feeding pit. Nate swallowed.

Aunt Phil unrolled a large wood and rope ladder that reached all the way down into the pit. "After you," she said.

Nate peered down. There were a number of gaping tunnels that opened onto the pit. *Those would be really good places for a wyvern to hide,* he thought. "Maybe you should go first so I can see how you climb down the ladder," he suggested.

Aunt Phil raised an eyebrow but went on ahead of him. Even though the ladder looked rickety, it seemed to hold her just fine. When it was Nate's turn, he sat on the edge of the cliff and scooted forward until his feet found the first rung.

"Be sure your helmet's secure," Aunt Phil called up to him. "It will protect your head if you fall."

Nate froze at the thought of tumbling all the way down. He looked longingly back over his shoulder. Why couldn't his last remaining relative have been a milkman or own a sweet shop? That would have been—

"Nate? Are you coming?"

"Yeah, I'm coming." He sighed, then gripped the sides of the ladder firmly. He turned around carefully so that he was now facing the cliff. Reaching down with his foot, he groped for the next rung.

The rope wobbled. A lot. Nate almost lost his grip more than once until Aunt Phil grabbed the bottom of the ladder and held it steady.

When he finally reached the ground, he blinked as his

eyes got used to the gloom. The air was dry and smelled musty. Bones and carcasses littered the floor of the cave, and he moved a little closer to Aunt Phil.

"Even wyverns can't eat bones," she explained. "Although they do make wonderful teething toys for them," she added thoughtfully.

When Aunt Phil stepped forward to inspect the four tunnels leading out of the pit, Greasle crawled out of the pack. "I wonder if there's any meat left on them bones?" the gremlin asked hopefully.

"Shh!" Nate warned her. "I'd be careful if I were you. She's still pretty peeved about the carrier pigeon."

"That wasn't my fault," Greasle muttered.

"Aha!" Aunt Phil said just then, surprising Nate. "The intruder took this path, which means he could wander for days before finding anything important. Excellent. If we hurry, we'll get to the wyverns before he does."

"What will we do with him once we find him?" Nate asked.

"That, dear boy, is a most excellent question. Here. This is the tunnel that leads to their main cavern," she said. And with no more warning than that, she stepped inside.

Nate took a deep breath, followed her into the tunnel, and stopped.

It was as if he had run into a wall of absolute blackness. He blinked and held his hand up to his face. Even though he knew it was there, he couldn't see a thing. The air was thick and warm and pressed down on him. Fear tried to claw its way up his throat. It felt as if the walls of the tunnel were moving closer, threatening to crush him.

"Lights on," Aunt Phil said cheerfully. There was a tiny snick of sound, and then a wide, bright beam of light penetrated the thick dark.

Nate heaved a sigh of relief and fumbled with his own helmet until his fingers found the switch. He flipped it on and a second beam of light flooded the tunnel. There still wasn't much to see except rock and— "What are you eating?" he asked Greasle.

She froze with a piece of shiny black rock halfway to her mouth. "Nothing," she said, whipping it behind her back.

Aunt Phil peered at her quizzically. "I believe she's found one of the many veins of coal that run through these mountains. Wales is rich with it. But I didn't realize gremlins could eat it. Do you like it?" she asked Greasle.

The gremlin took another bite and chewed thoughtfully. "I do. It's crunchy but tastes a bit like engines."

"Fascinating," Aunt Phil murmured. "Well, eat all you like. You can't hurt anything down here."

Greasle's ears perked up and she broke off another piece of coal from the wall, munching as they continued on their way.

"Will we be able to sneak up on the wyverns with these lights?" Nate asked.

"Oh, there was never any chance of our sneaking up on them. They'll smell us long before we see them. Chances are, *they'll* sneak up on *us*. It'll be a good opportunity for them to practice their hunting skills, no doubt."

Nate stopped walking. "They're going to practice on us? I thought you said we were protected by the Covenant?"

"They're too young to understand about the Covenant. And even if they did, young wyverns have very poor impulse control. They probably wouldn't remember the agreement until after they'd attacked us and gotten in trouble for it."

Wonderful, Nate thought.

In spite of the lanterns, it was slow going. The light exposed only bits and pieces of the path ahead, which twisted

and turned and seemed to loop back on itself. Every so often, they would pass a gaping hole in the wall that led to yet another tunnel.

The ground was rough and Nate stumbled over rocks and debris half a dozen times. Once, he tripped over a bone of some kind and nearly landed on his face.

At the next bend in the tunnel, Nate's light fell on something long and fluttering. *A ghost?* He jumped back. "What's that?" he asked.

"It's only dragon skin. As they grow, they shed their skins. Here, come have a closer look."

Nate followed her over to the dragon skin. Up close, it shimmered faintly in the beams of light. There was a rainbow sheen to it.

"Touch it, Nate," Aunt Phil said.

He did. It was soft and feathery against his fingers.

"You can take a bit for your collection if you'd like."

Nate looked at her in surprise. He didn't realize she'd noticed the few specimens he'd collected. "Thanks," he said.

The skin was surprisingly tough. He couldn't tear it with his hands, so Aunt Phil handed him a small pocketknife. "Try this."

The small sharp blade sliced cleanly through the dragon skin. When he went to hand it back to her, she shook her head. "No, you keep it. I have others and you might need one down here."

"Really? I'm allowed to have my own knife?" he asked, not quite believing her.

"You're a beastologist-in-training now. Of course you need the proper tools."

Nate started to smile, then stopped. "But will a pocket-knife be of any use against wyverns?" he asked.

"Goodness, no!" Aunt Phil said. "It's not to use on them. It's in case you get stuck or have to cut something loose. You're never to use it on a wyvern."

"Oh." Nate stuffed the piece of dragon skin into one of the outside pockets of his rucksack. He held on to the knife as they continued on their way. He liked the solid feel of it in his hand.

Two twists and turns later, Nate's light fell on a dozen small, slithering shapes. He leaped back against the cavern wall. "Are those the babies?"

"They're much too small, Nate. They're salamanders."

"Salamanders?" he repeated.

"Yes, elemental creatures of fire. They're attracted to the wyverns' flames. If you see them, you know the wyverns are very near."

Nate gulped and knelt down so he could see them better. "They're kind of cute."

Sensing his body's warmth, they clustered around his hand. Their tiny feet tickled. One brave salamander had just crawled all the way onto the back of Nate's wrist when a deep roar boomed through the tunnel. The salamanders scattered.

"I believe we've found the wyverns," Aunt Phil announced.

Chapter Ten

*N*ATE'S FIRST GLIMPSE of a young wyvern turned out to be a long, twitching tail. He nearly stepped on it as he crept around the next bend.

His first thought was *They didn't smell us after all.* However, that was chased from his mind as the wyvern in front of him roared and launched forward. There was a deep squeak as the beast landed on another wyvern, the one he'd been sneaking up on. They growled and rolled on the floor, emitting loud grumbles and spitting fire. Nate leaped back out of the way of the flames and flailing tails. Greasle squealed, scampered up his leg, then dove into the safety of the pack.

"These are two-year-olds. Juvies, we call them," Aunt Phil whispered. "Aren't they cute, practicing their hunting skills like that?"

Nate turned to stare at her. She was smiling at them as if they were nothing but a litter of kittens playing with a ball of yarn. Had she lost her mind?

There were five of them, and they were about the same size as a giraffe Nate had seen at a zoo once. Their eyes were yellow, with red slits in the middle that flickered like flames. Their teeth were much smaller than the adults', but still very sharp looking. Their wings were nothing but useless little stubs on their back.

As they broke apart, the largest one stuck his snout in the air and sniffed.

"Best get your ear trumpet in place," Aunt Phil told Nate.

What he really wanted was to grab his pick and hold it out in front of him, but he didn't think Aunt Phil would approve. Instead, he quickly unhooked his ear trumpet from his belt. He stuck it in his ear just in time to hear the young wyvern's words. "I sssmell something."

The other wyverns stopped their roughhousing and lifted their snouts into the air as well. Then they all turned toward Aunt Phil and Nate.

As loud as they had been before, they were now eerily

quiet, creeping closer. Their long pink tongues flicked out, testing the air.

"Not too close, now," Aunt Phil warned. "We come in peace. Your parents have agreed to parley with us, so we are granted free passage."

"Parsssley?" the closest wyvern repeated. "Isn't that the tasty green stuff Mum puts on sheep?"

"No, par*ley*," Aunt Phil repeated, saying the word very slowly. "It is an agreement between your parents and us to try to solve problems before taking action."

"Who are you?"

"I'm a beastologist."

The smallest one perked up. "Beasts? We eat beasts."

"Not beastologists, you don't," Aunt Phil said firmly.

The smallest was very close to Nate now. His long tongue flicked out and touched Nate's face. Nate jerked back.

"Isss salty," the young wyvern announced to the others. "Not as fuzzy as sheep."

"Stop that, now," Aunt Phil scolded. "We've important work to do here. Have you seen any other humans? Creatures who look like us?"

"No," the largest wyvern said as he moved closer. "Only you."

"Shoo," Aunt Phil said, flapping her hands at them. "Shoo."

But unlike the crocodiles of the Niger River, *shoo* didn't seem to work on the wyverns. In fact, if anything, they drew closer.

"Why aren't they listening?" Nate asked, backing away. "They have ears, don't they?"

The nearest juvie moved even closer and cocked his head to the side. "Wasss that a riddle?" he asked, twirling his tail.

"Brilliant idea, Nate, appealing to their higher nature like that," Aunt Phil told him. "Riddles stimulate their intellect."

Nate swallowed. "Um, that wasn't a riddle. That was a question."

"Oh. Well, best get the pennies out, then."

The juvies took another step forward. Nate gulped and reached for his pocket. Just then, a bell sounded, a clean, clanging series of notes in the distance.

Every single wyvern froze, then trundled off toward the

sound. Nate, Aunt Phil, and Greasle were suddenly alone in the corridor. "Dewey and his dinner bell," Aunt Phil explained.

Nate remembered the large bell that hung on the wall back in the first cavern and Dewey's insistence that he would feed the wyverns later. Nate was heartily grateful. "But why would they leave us for a stupid old bell?" he asked, falling into step behind Aunt Phil.

"Ah, we learned that trick from the experiments of a Russian named Pavlov. He did a fascinating experiment with dogs. Every time he fed these dogs, he'd ring a bell. After a while, the dogs always reacted to the sound of a bell as if it were feeding time. Shortly after that, Dewey and I spent a few months training the juvies to the sound of a bell. We placed one in the main cavern and one in the feeding pit. We figured it would be a handy way to be able to call them all at once when we wished to take a head count. It's turned out to be more useful than I ever could have imagined. Now whenever they hear that bell they come running, knowing they will be fed. Ah, here we are. The main cavern."

Nate stepped out of the tunnel and into the main cavern,

his jaw dropping open in surprise. It was no gloomy, dark hidey-hole. It was . . . beautiful.

The stone was smooth and polished, not all crumbly and bumpy like the tunnel had been. Long, delicate spires of crystallized minerals hung down from the rocks, like decorations on a fancy chandelier.

The ceiling went up for miles, it seemed, until it disappeared into the top of the mountain. Halfway up, there was a large opening and a shelf. As Nate, Aunt Phil, and Greasle gazed upward, a large adult wyvern swooped in through the opening and dived toward the floor of the cave.

Chapter Eleven

"COME WATCH THIS." Aunt Phil grabbed Nate's arm and pulled him back toward the wall. Not out of sight, exactly, but out of the way.

As the wyvern landed on the cavern floor, half a dozen babies swarmed toward it. When they reached the adult, the bigger beast began to cough. Or choke. Or— "Why is he trying to throw up on them?" Nate asked.

Aunt Phil glanced at him. "*She's* not throwing up, Nate. She's regurgitating food for them. All wyverns are fiercely devoted parents. They don't nurse their young like mammals do. Instead, they chew and partially digest food for the hatchlings, then regurgitate it so their young mouths can manage it. At least until their teeth come in."

Ew, was all Nate could think. Even Greasle said, "That's disgusting, that is!"

But the baby wyverns seemed very pleased with their meal. And Nate was surprised at how gentle and loving the adult wyvern was toward them. He'd never thought of a dragon in quite that way.

When the wyvern had finished feeding the babies, she turned her giant head toward Nate and Aunt Phil. Nate jumped back and plastered himself against the cave wall. "Don't worry," Aunt Phil said. "She knows about the parley. Trumpets in place," she reminded him. Nate fumbled at his belt and got his ear trumpet unhooked.

"Greetingsss, doctor."

"Greetings, Nerys. Have you seen any sign of an intruder during your feeding duties?"

The wyvern lifted her snout and sniffed the air. "No, but I can ssstill smell him."

"Onward, then," Aunt Phil said.

"Before you leave," Nerys said. "Would you take a look

in the hatchery? There is one lone egg that will not hatch. We would like you to look at it, if you don't mind."

"I'd be glad to. Come on, Nate." She led him to a small cave off the main cavern.

The minute Nate stepped inside, he began to sweat. "Why is it so hot in here?"

Aunt Phil pointed to a small, bubbling pool. "It's an underground hot springs. Wyverns are much too heavy to sit on their eggs. They would break immediately. And if the shell were thick enough to withstand their weight, a baby wyvern would never be able to break through. The warm air helps keep the eggs warm until they hatch. The moisture keeps them from hardening too soon."

Nate saw one lone egg propped up on a sad little pile of hay. It stood nearly two feet tall, and Greasle licked her lips. "Just think of the heaping plate of strangled eggs that would make!" she said.

"*Scram*bled. It's *scrambled* eggs, not strangled. And yuck."

Aunt Phil reached the egg and knelt down to examine it. "Come here, Nate. This is an excellent opportunity for you to see an egg up close."

As he drew next to her, he saw that the egg was covered

in a soft sheen of colors that changed slightly whenever he moved his head. "Touch it," Aunt Phil instructed.

He glanced over his shoulder to see if Nerys was watching. She was tending to the babies, so he reached out and laid one finger on the egg. It was warm and smooth. He started to pull his hand away, but Aunt Phil stopped him. "Now tap it with your fingernail. But no more than a tap— we don't want to risk cracking it before it's ready."

"Why not?"

"Well, there are two reasons. One, the hatchling won't be strong enough to survive if he doesn't build his muscles while struggling to get out. And two, we don't want it imprinting on us. Whoever the hatchling sees first becomes its parent. That happened to Morris Fludd, back in 1716. He ended up having to move into the caves with the wyverns and spent the rest of his life in here with them. Luckily, he was a dedicated beastologist, so he didn't mind. Much."

Nate did as she instructed, giving three little taps with his finger. It made a faint *clack, clack, clack* sound.

"When you hear that sound, you know the shell has fully hardened and is ready to hatch. But for some reason, this one hasn't."

"How long does it take a wyvern egg to hatch?" Nate asked.

"There are many factors involved: The temperature, for one. What its mother ate before laying it, her age and overall health. The weather also plays a large role. Eggs take longer to hatch in wet, rainy years than they do in dry ones.

"And of course, it also depends on the dragonling inside the egg. How big he is, how strong, how aggressive. Truthfully, there are dozens of factors, which is why it can take anywhere from twelve to fourteen months. However, every once in a while there is a dud. I suspect this egg has begun to harden simply because it is drying out, not because it is getting ready to hatch."

"That's sad," Nate said.

"Yes, it is. And with so few of them left, every wyvern is precious to us. But sometimes these things can't be helped."

"What happens to the egg if it doesn't hatch?"

"The insides harden and turn to crystal, and the outsides become more and more rocklike. When the parents are certain the egg won't hatch, they take the dud to a pit a short ways away. Many people collect them. Having no idea what they truly are, they call them geodes."

Nate studied the egg, marveling at the satiny smooth feel of it. It seemed hardly fair to dump it into a pit just because it was slow to hatch. He'd been slow to hatch, too. His parents had completely given up on his Fludd skills. It was only because Aunt Phil believed in him that he'd been given a second chance. "No," he said, surprising both himself and Aunt Phil. Maybe this egg needed a second chance, too. "Let's give it a little longer."

"Nate," Aunt Phil said gently. "Sometimes eggs won't hatch no matter how long we give them."

"Still," he said stubbornly. "What can it hurt?"

She studied his face, and he knew she was thinking of his parents. "Very well. We'll give it a few more hours." She turned and left the hatchery. Feeling better, Nate gave the egg one last pat, then followed his aunt back into the main cavern.

"Nerys," Aunt Phil called up to the adult wyvern. "We've decided it is probably a dud, but it won't hurt to give it a bit longer."

The great wyvern nodded her head, then launched herself up to the opening.

"Now," Aunt Phil said, all brisk business, "we've got to

locate that intruder before he gets a chance to make any mischief. Hang on while I consult the cavern map to see which route will allow us to intercept him." She swung her pack off her back, muttering something about inconvenience, then drew *The Book of Beasts* from it. As she studied the map, Nate pulled his sketchbook out, perched himself on a small rock, and began to draw the baby wyverns.

The yearlings were rolling and tumbling in a pile. They were about the size of the crocodiles they'd run into at the Niger River, but they were cuter somehow. Their skin was much smoother and iridescent. Their eyes were big and weren't roiling and boiling like the adults' or juvies'. As Nate looked into their faces, he saw that the babies were happy and fed and curious about him.

"Okay, Nate. I've got it," Aunt Phil said, swinging the pack back up onto her shoulders. "Let's move out."

Nate hastily put his sketchbook away.

"This is the tunnel we need," she said, then headed off into the looming darkness.

Chapter Twelve

*T*HEY HEARD *OBEDIAH* before they saw him. He was huffing and puffing his way down the corridor, grumbling under his breath. "Why do wyverns need so many tunnels anyway? Why not a nice big cage so I wouldn't have to go hunting around for them? When I'm in charge, that's what it'll be. A cage, so I don't have to search for the blighters—*oof*."

Aunt Phil stepped from her hiding place so suddenly that Obediah plowed right into her. Knocked off balance, he fell to the ground. "Greetings, cousin," she said coolly.

Obediah blinked owlishly in the light from her helmet. He put his hand up to shield his eyes. "Philomena? Is that you? What are you doing here?"

"Funny," Aunt Phil said. "I should be asking you that question."

"What do you mean?"

"I mean, what are you up to? First you try to steal *The Book of Beasts*, then you let loose one of the deadliest beasts known to man, and then you break into my house and search it. Why?"

"What makes you think I was in Africa? Or broke into your house, for that matter?" he asked, his voice squeaking a bit.

"You match the description given. And now we find you skulking around in the wyverns' caves causing an uproar."

He rubbed his hands together nervously. "I just wanted to have a small peek at the dragons, that's all. Then I got lost. Didn't think I'd ever find my way out."

Aunt Phil folded her arms and studied him. "Is that so?"

He nodded his head. "Oh yes. It's all true. Every word."

"You wanted to see the wyverns immediately after visiting the basilisk?"

Obediah pushed to his feet. "Uh, well. It was a pilgrimage, you see. To get in touch with my Fludd heritage."

"But your branch of the family has shown no sign of interest in our doings for centuries."

"But that doesn't mean it's too late, does it?" He smiled, a fake, oily smile that Nate didn't like one bit. "You're not refusing a fellow Fludd a chance to come back into the fold, are you? There are so few of us left these days."

"If you are so anxious to reconcile, why did you ransack my house?"

Obediah licked his lips. "I have no idea what you're talking about. I'm sure I've never been to your house before. Why, I don't even know where it is!"

Don't believe him, Nate thought. *Don't believe him*. Nate studied Aunt Phil's face, unable to tell what she was thinking.

Aunt Phil folded her arms and studied Obediah. "What I really want to know is how you were able to locate the beasts—"

Her question was interrupted by a loud roar. It sounded very close. "Oh dear. The juvies have finished their dinner.

This is not the time or place to have this conversation, but we *will* have it. Soon. Once we're out of the caverns."

Nate wanted to scream, *What about my parents?*

"Of course, cousin," Obediah said. "I am most anxious to repair relations between the branches of our families. I'll be happy to answer any questions once you get us out of here safely. I find I'm not all that fond of enclosed spaces." Obediah gave another sickly smile.

As Aunt Phil began to lead the way, Obediah followed, with Nate bringing up the rear. Greasle wriggled up out of the pack. "I don't likes him," she whispered to Nate.

"I don't either," he whispered back. "And I don't believe a single word he says."

Chapter Thirteen

N_{ATE} $_{COULDN'T}$ $_{TELL}$ if Aunt Phil was buying Obediah's explanation or not, so he decided to take matters into his own hands. He quickened his pace until he was walking beside Obediah. "So," Nate asked, watching the man closely, "how *did* you know where to find all the beasts? Aunt Phil says they're pretty hard to find."

Obediah stared down at him as if he were a wyvern dropping. "You heard the woman. She said we'll talk about it later."

"What's the matter, you big oaf?" Greasle piped up. "Can't you walk and talk at the same time?"

"Of course I can," Obediah snarled. Then he blinked and looked closer at Greasle. "You?" he asked, rubbing the bite marks on his hand.

"Yeah, me. And I knows when I taste a dirty rotten liar."

Obediah's eyes narrowed and he flexed his hand. Afraid he was going to hit Greasle, Nate scampered to catch up to Aunt Phil. He grabbed her arm and pulled her forward so that Obediah couldn't hear them. "He did something to my parents," he whispered.

"We don't know that for certain," Aunt Phil whispered back. "While he is a despicable person and up to no good, we can't accuse him of kidnapping and murder without any proof. You're letting your imagination run away with you."

Nate wanted to argue, but they reached the main cavern just then. Obediah stopped in his tracks. His eyes lit up and searched the cavern hungrily. "Is this where they keep the treasure?" he asked innocently.

Aunt Phil's eyes narrowed. "Was your pilgrimage for the wyverns or their treasure?" she asked.

"The wyverns. Of course." He licked his lips. "But even

so, I imagine their treasure would be wondrous to behold."

"Well, you're out of luck, I'm afraid. It's kept in another part of the caverns. But here are those wyverns you were so anxious to see."

Obediah turned in the direction Aunt Phil was pointing, his eyes widening in alarm. Curious, the yearlings crept over to explore him.

Obediah backed up against the wall. One yearling drew closer, then flicked its skinny little tongue out to smell him better.

Obediah kicked it in the snout. The baby wyvern squealed, and Aunt Phil shouted, "NO!" She grabbed Obediah's arm and pulled him away. "What do you think you're doing?"

"Protecting myself," Obediah said defiantly.

"Against what? They're harmless. They've no venom—no wyverns have venom—and their fire-breathing skills haven't come in yet. They can't even take a bite out of you." Aunt Phil hurried over to the yearling's side and knelt beside it. "I'm sorry. That idiot man didn't mean to hurt you. He's just ignorant." After a moment, the yearling rubbed his head against Aunt Phil's shoulder and began to—

"Purr?" Obediah squawked. "Dragons purr?"

"Of course they purr," Aunt Phil snapped. "That's how they communicate pleasure. Now let's get going before you set human and wyvern relations back a thousand years."

"Before we go, can I check on the egg?" Nate asked.

"Yes, but quickly."

As Nate headed for the hatchery, Obediah fell into step behind him. "An egg?" he asked. "Is there really a dragon egg? Can I see it, too?" he asked.

"If you have to," Nate mumbled. Deciding it was best to ignore Obediah, Nate hurried over to the egg and knelt beside it. The pearly sheen hadn't changed any, nor were there any signs of a crack. He gently tapped the egg. *Clack, clack, clack.* Then he put his ear against it.

Thunk!

He gasped, his eyes widening in surprise. He gently tapped again. This time he distinctly heard a faint scratch. He turned to shout the news to Aunt Phil, then felt a hard tug on his pack that yanked him back onto his behind.

"I'll take that, if you please."

Nate blinked. Obediah had grabbed Nate's pick and now held it over the egg. Not only that, but his whole manner had changed. Gone was the bumbling fool and in his place was a sly, cunning, dangerous-looking man. He stood over Nate, gloating and triumphant.

"I've got a powerful urge to see just what's inside this egg. I think I'll . . ." He raised the pick, and Nate shouted, "NO!"

Obediah cocked his head to the side. "What? You don't want to see what's inside?"

Nate stared at him silently, unsure what to do.

"On your feet. We'll go tell your aunt there's been a change of plans, shall we? I'm not ready to leave."

Once Nate was standing, Obediah prodded him in the back with the pick. Nate marched forward. When they appeared in the main cavern, Aunt Phil stopped petting a baby wyvern and slowly got to her feet. "What's going on?"

"There's been a slight change of plans, I'm afraid. I'm not quite done here. I have a treasure to find and I'm not leaving until I do."

"Treasure?" Aunt Phil repeated. "I'm afraid you're mistaken. The wyverns' treasure is nothing but baubles and trinkets. There is nothing of any real value—"

"Quiet!" Obediah brandished the pick at Nate. "I wouldn't expect you to tell me where the good stuff is. But the time has come for our branch to have a piece of the spoils. Now come on over here and tie the boy up."

Her eyes on the sharp point of the pick, Aunt Phil came over to Nate's side.

"Go on, tie him up. Hands and feet."

"Sorry, Nate," Aunt Phil muttered. She took the rope from his pack and began tying his wrists.

Obediah watched them closely. "Don't try to fool me. I want good, tight knots."

Aunt Phil sighed and retied the knot. When Nate was secured, Obediah told Aunt Phil to take off her pack and lay it on the ground. Keeping his eyes on her the whole time, he snatched the rope from her pack and ordered her to turn around.

When she was trussed up like a Christmas goose, he cackled. "I don't think you'll be needing this any longer." He lifted her pack from the ground and waved it triumphantly before placing it on his own shoulders.

With horror, Nate thought of *The Book of Beasts*. And the

cavern map! Both were in Aunt Phil's pack. They'd never find their way out, even if they could get untied.

"Thanks for showing me the way to the main cavern. I might not ever have found it on my own." He turned and headed back to the tunnel they'd found him in. As he passed a dinner bell, he paused. He glanced over his shoulder at Nate and Aunt Phil, then reached up and rang the bell before disappearing down the tunnel.

Chapter Fourteen

THE MINUTE OBEDIAH was out of sight, Aunt Phil began struggling against her bonds.

"How long until the wyverns get here?" Nate asked, testing his knots. They held tight.

"A minute or two, depending on how far away they were to start with. Bother!" she said. "The man does know how to tie knots, even if he is a disgrace to the Fludd name."

Nate twisted his head, trying to see his backpack. "Greasle? Do you think you could help us out here?"

"Is that nasty man gones?" she asked from the safety of the pack.

"Yeah, he's gone."

"Okay, then." She scrambled out of the pack and scampered up onto his shoulder. "Whatcha need?"

"Could you untie us?"

She squinted down at the ropes on his wrists. "Did he do this to yous?"

"Yeah."

"Knew I didn't likes him," she said, then scampered down his arm—which tickled—and began undoing the knots with her small, nimble fingers.

"Thank you," Nate said, rubbing his wrists. "I'll take care of my feet while you untie Aunt Phil."

Greasle shook her head.

Nate frowned and nodded toward Aunt Phil. "Go on. She won't bite," he whispered.

Ears back in fear, Greasle approached Aunt Phil. Aunt Phil squatted down so that Greasle could reach her wrists and waited patiently. While the little gremlin untied the rope, Nate reached for the knots at his ankles. But his fingers were nowhere near as tiny or quick as the gremlin's.

He let go of the rope and got his new pocketknife out. Very carefully, he inserted the tip of the knife between the rope and his ankles. Then he sliced it in one quick, clean cut. It fell to the ground just as Greasle finished untying Aunt Phil. His aunt stood up. "Thank you, Greasle. Very much."

The gremlin turned and gaped at Nate. That was the nicest thing Aunt Phil had ever said to her.

"Best put that knife away and get your pennies out. Here come the juvies, and they'll be expecting food," Aunt Phil warned.

Nate slipped his knife into one of his pockets, then reached for the pennies with the other hand. The cold, hard feel of them was comforting against his palm.

Grunts and squeaks and the sound of sharp talons clattering on rock echoed around them. The juvies burst into the main cavern, a whirling confusion of wings, tails, and snouts. The young wyverns quickly caught Nate's and Aunt Phil's scents and turned in their direction.

"Into the pool, I think," Aunt Phil said. "Fishing the pennies out will keep them occupied just that much longer. One, two, three, *now!*"

Nate flung his pennies with all his might. The flashing copper shine of them caught the juvies' attention. Their gazes fastened on the treasure.

"Now," Aunt Phil whispered, "let's get out of here."

As they disappeared into the tunnel, Nate heard a splash as the first of the juvies hit the water.

Luckily, Obediah hadn't thought to take their lantern helmets. "How will we find our way out of here now that he has *The Book of Beasts* with the cavern map?" Nate asked.

Aunt Phil smiled and patted the front of her shirt. "Actually, I still have it. I slipped it into here because I got tired of having to stop and take it out of the pack every time I wanted to look at it. So Obediah doesn't have a map. Which will allow us to catch up to him before he reaches the treasury."

Nate fell into step behind Aunt Phil. Greasle climbed out to ride on his shoulder. "Okay, but why do we care if he gets to the treasure? Didn't you say it was just a bunch of shiny old junk anyway?"

"Mostly, although there are some truly valuable bits left over from centuries gone by. But that's not what I'm worried about. What Obediah doesn't know is that the treasury is in the wyverns' inner sanctum, their most holy of holies. It's where old wyverns go to die, their tired bones and joints comforted by the warmth thrown off by the shine of the treasure. Obediah is walking straight into Old Nudd, a truly ancient wyvern with a very sour disposition."

"Why is he so grumpy?" Nate asked.

"It's a sad story, really. I'm afraid his mate disappeared more than a year ago. As best we can tell, she fell in love with a passing zeppelin and followed it out of sight."

"I thought you said wyverns mate for life?"

"They do. That's why this was so distressing for all concerned. Nudd searched high and low, but with no luck. When he returned, his old heart was broken. He's been waiting to die ever since. He will not show any mercy with an intruder."

"Seems to me likes that man deserves his fate," Greasle said.

"Normally I would agree with you," Aunt Phil said. This

surprised the gremlin so much, she nearly fell off Nate's shoulder. He had to put his hand up to steady her.

"However, if a human invades the wyverns' inner sanctum, the wyverns have the right to demand their life as a penalty."

Greasle harrumphed. "They'd attack us for certain if they saw how nasty that man tastes."

Not to mention, Nate would never get to ask Obediah about his parents.

Chapter Fifteen

AUNT PHIL CONSULTED THE CAVE MAP twice more before she finally put it away.

"How will we know which way Obediah went?" Nate asked.

"We won't. My goal is to park ourselves in front of the treasury and snag him when he shows up."

They walked along in silence, twisting and turning their way deeper into the mountain. Nate lost all track of time and direction. Just when he was certain they'd reached the very center of the earth itself, an enormous roar blasted through the caves.

"Looks like Obediah's found Old Nudd," Aunt Phil said grimly. "Come on!" She broke into a run.

Nate followed, holding Greasle in place so she wouldn't bounce off his shoulder. Aunt Phil stopped abruptly in front of a downward-sloping tunnel. A very pale golden glow shone at the bottom.

"Here we are," she said. "Now listen carefully." She fumbled with the front of her shirt and pulled something out. "Here is *The Book of Beasts*. I want you to have it for safe-keeping. If anything happens to me, you'll have everything you need to be the next beastologist."

"No!" Nate said, horrified. "Nothing is going to happen to you!"

"It probably won't, but just in case. Remember, we have a responsibility to the animals we care for. Now, here's my watch. If I'm not out in half an hour, leave. Get out. Do not try to rescue me. This isn't like Arabia, where you could bargain for my safety. Wyverns are very sly and clever when they want to be and you'll only be walking into a

trap." She put her hands on Nate's shoulders. "Take care, my boy." She gave him a quick kiss on the forehead, then disappeared down into the cave tunnel.

No, he wanted to shout. *Come back!* But he couldn't. It was her duty—his duty now, too—to take care of these beasts. He slumped down onto the cave floor to wait, his eyes glued to the watch. One minute went by. Two. Sick with worry, he found he couldn't sit still. He got to his feet and began pacing.

"Could you stop that? You're making me dizzy," Greasle complained.

Nate ignored her, so she hopped off his shoulder and waited on the floor. He could hear sounds coming from down below. Loud rumbles and snorts and the faint sound of voices, but he couldn't make out the words. He checked the watch again. Shook it. Only ten minutes had passed. He strained to make out what the voices were saying. He even put the trumpet to his ear, trying to make out the wyvern's words. But they were too garbled from this distance.

It was truly the longest half hour of his life.

The minute hand inched

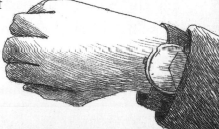

past the thirty-minute mark. *Come back come back come back*, he wished, with all his might. Willed it to be so.

But no one came.

He stared down the long empty tunnel, hoping against hope he'd see Aunt Phil striding toward him.

"Come on." Greasle tugged at his knee. "We's got to gets out of here, like she said."

"I can't just leave her," Nate groaned.

"Sure you can," Greasle said. "She told you to."

"You don't understand. She's the only one left." The only one who cared about him. The only one who could help him learn what had happened to his parents. Even more, he'd come to care very deeply about her. Thoughts and fears scrambled around in his head in a vicious tangle. Finally, he made a decision. "I'm going in," he said.

"No!" squeaked Greasle.

"Yes. But if you want to wait here, you can."

"All alone? With them juvies roaming around? I don't think so," she snorted, then hopped up onto his shoulder and climbed into his pack. "Wake me when it's over."

"Will do." Nate squared his shoulders, lifted his trembling chin, and headed for the treasury.

Chapter Sixteen

JUST INSIDE THE CAVE OPENING, the narrow tunnel wound downward until it opened up into a huge cavern, nearly as big as the main one. In the warm, glowing light coming off the treasure, Nate saw Obediah and Aunt Phil backed up against the far wall, trapped by a long, lashing tail.

"Nate! No!" Aunt Phil yelled.

The enormous wyvern whipped his head around, his red roiling gaze nailing Nate in place.

Old Nudd's head was huge. Possibly bigger than Nate himself. The scales on his scarred face were crusty with age.

The wyvern roared, a loud rumble of sound that pounded against Nate's ears. He quickly shoved his ear trumpet in place.

"—or should I say offering?" the wyvern was saying. "For any that wander into this realm are surely an offering to

me." The wyvern chortled, the most horrid and unnerving sound Nate had ever heard.

"He's not an offering!" Aunt Phil yelled, her voice frantic. "He's just a child. You can't harm a child!"

"No?" Nudd asked. "Does it say that sssomewhere in your precious Covenant? That our rules apply to everyone, except for children?"

"No, but it should." Aunt Phil looked at Nate helplessly. "Besides, he's the next beastologist, and there are always exceptions for beastologists."

Nate gulped. His plan, which hadn't been very good to start with, now seemed especially puny. "I-I brought you some treasure," he said. "T-to trade for my aunt." Nate held up the cherished Fludd compass that Aunt Phil had given him just a short time ago and his pocketknife. He hated to part with them, but they were the only shiny things he owned.

The wyvern roared, sending a billow of smoke in Nate's direction and covering him in ash. "Don't need more trea-surrrre . . ."

The wyvern had a point, Nate thought, studying the pile of treasure Old Nudd sat on. He probably didn't need any more. But even with all the treasure and the warmth it threw off, the cavern seemed huge and empty to Nate. And then he had an idea. A great, big, wonderful idea.

He cleared his throat. "I have a greater treasure you might like, but I have to go get it."

"Why should I let you go and risssk losing my prize?" Old Nudd grumbled.

"Because the treasure I will bring you will last a whole lifetime."

The dragon snorted again, sending another little puff of smoke Nate's way. But there was a spark of curiosity in his eyes. Nate was sure of it. "Are you offering me a riddle?" Nudd asked.

"Yes," Nate said. "I am. What treasure shines brighter than gold and lasts a lifetime?"

Old Nudd narrowed his eyes and showed the first sign of true interest. Nate waited, holding his breath.

"Hmm . . ." Nudd grumbled, sounding less angry. "Very well. For the sssake of this riddle I cannot answer, I will let you fetch thisss treasure. But hurry." He lifted one of his claws and inspected the point. "I am afraid I grow hungry."

Chapter Seventeen

NATE TORE OUT OF THE CAVE, panic nipping at his heels. Would it work? He could only hope.

His feet pounded along the hard rock floor, his head lantern bobbing and weaving as the tunnel climbed up and up and finally leveled off. He paused and closed his eyes, trying to retrace the steps in his mind. They'd turned left, left, right, and then left. Which meant he had to go right, right, left, then right. Hoping he'd remembered correctly, he took off at a run. Relieved when he reached the main cavern, he paused long enough to check for juvies, but there were none in sight. He quickly headed for the hatchery, then slowly approached the sole remaining egg.

There were more cracks now, dozens of them covering the surface. The trick would be to get the egg back to the treasury before it hatched. Nate needed the dragonling to imprint on Old Nudd, not him.

It was too big to fit into his pack. And too heavy for him to carry. If he rolled it, the shell would crack open for sure. He swung his pack off his shoulders and put it on the ground. As he was untying his bedroll, Greasle poked her head out. "Did that weirdvern eat that old lady yet?"

"No," Nate said.

Seeing no one else about, the gremlin crawled all the way out of the pack. "Whatcha doin'?"

"I'm trying to figure out a way to get this egg to the treasury. I think this bedroll will work like a sling, and I can drag it back." It would take a long time, and he'd have to be careful about bumps along the way, but it might work. It was the only thing he could think of. Using great care, he placed the cracking egg in the middle of the bedroll.

"Why'd you want to do that?"

"I'm hoping Old Nudd will be so happy for some company that he'll let Aunt Phil and Obediah go free." When the egg was centered, Nate wrapped the corners of the bedroll up around it and gave a gentle tug. It seemed to work.

Greasle shook her head. "He seemed awful grouchy to me. What makes you think he wants any company?"

Nate hoisted the ends of the bedroll over his shoulder and glared at Greasle. "If you're not going to help, then get back in the pack."

In the end, Greasle scampered along in front of him as he began making the slow, careful journey back to the treasury. Every bump in the ground, every pile of rocks, threatened to crack the egg wide open. But he was very careful, always moving slowly to ease his burden over the bumpy parts. Greasle made herself useful by calling out a warning when there were large rocks or bumps up ahead.

Nate's arms were shaking and he was covered in sweat by the time he finally reached the treasury. Feeling nervous and uncertain, Nate dragged the egg the last few feet until it sat right in front of Nudd.

The old wyvern roared, the force of his voice setting the treasure underneath him to rattling. Nate got his ear trumpet in place in time to hear Nudd ask, "What do I want with an old dud of an egg?" He roared again and lashed his tail, narrowly missing Aunt Phil and Obediah.

"But it's not a dud," Nate said in a small voice. "Look."

Old Nudd lowered his head and nudged the egg with one long claw.

Nate held his breath, afraid to be so close to the wyvern, yet more afraid to move away.

"How do I know you didn't crack it on the way here?"

"Why would I lie to a wyvern?" Nate asked. "Besides, if you listen carefully, you can hear something moving inside."

Old Nudd turned his head, bringing his long narrow snout and sharp teeth even closer to Nate as he put his ear right next to the egg and listened. At that very same moment, a small claw burst through the shell and poked Old Nudd in the cheek. He snorted a billow of smoke and jerked back, blinking in surprise.

Sensing freedom now, the hatchling began wriggling in earnest. An entire leg kicked through, then a snout. A spiny wing poked out of the top and then finally, with a loud crack, the egg shattered. The pieces fell onto the cave floor, all except for one that balanced precariously on the hatchling's head, like a hat.

As the baby wyvern opened its eyes, Nate flung himself to the ground, terrified it would imprint on him instead of Old Nudd.

Nate peered up through his fingers. The baby was still wet from all the egg goo that covered its skin, and its wings were flattened to its back. It looked slightly befuddled, then turned to Old Nudd and brightened. *"Grok?"*

Old Nudd sniffed. "She's rather puny," he said, not fooling anyone.

Aunt Phil stepped away from the wall and stood next to Nate.

"All infants are," she pointed out.

Old Nudd rolled his eyes and sighed, sending a massive plume of smoke toward the baby. "I suppose you expect me to clean it up."

The baby wyvern meeped. She tried to take a step toward

Nudd, but her legs got tangled up in the pieces of shell and she ended up in a heap on the floor.

Nudd sighed and hooked one long talon under the baby's wings and lifted her to her feet. Nate felt like cheering.

The thing was, as angry and scary as Old Nudd was, Nate had sensed an overwhelming misery and loneliness in him. Nate recognized it because it was exactly how he felt when he woke up in the middle of the night and remembered that his parents and Miss Lumpton were gone. Suddenly, fiercely, Nate had wanted to fix it. He had wanted to find a way to not just get Aunt Phil free, but to take away Old Nudd's loneliness. And he'd remembered the egg.

The baby was back on her feet now and Nudd gingerly picked off the last remaining bit of shell. The infant meeped again, then *grokked*. Old Nudd's face softened and a low, rumbling growl emerged from his chest. It took Nate a full minute to realize he was purring.

Then Nudd's long tongue flicked out and began cleaning the egg slime from the baby's skin. The baby squirmed in pleasure and meeped again, this time scooting forward to rub against Nudd's leg. "She is a very handsome hatchling, is she not?" the old wyvern said.

"Beautiful," Nate agreed, hiding his smile. "What will you name her?"

Old Nudd considered. "I will call her Belli, because she shines so brightly." Then he turned to Nate. "You were right. This treasure is more valuable than any gold and will lassst a lifetime. You have earned freedom for all of you."

Belli *grokked*, and Nudd turned his attention back to the dragonling.

"Well done, Nate!" Nate glanced up to find Aunt Phil beaming at him. She looked happy enough to reach out and lick him, just like Old Nudd had done. Nate took a step back, just in case. "Thanks," he said, pleased.

They watched Nudd and Belli for a few more moments. Deep inside, Nate felt a glowing satisfaction, and something else, too. A longing. He glanced over at Aunt Phil, whose face was still beaming.

"Aunt Phil," he began.

"Yes, Nate?" She reached up and hastily wiped a tear from the corner of her eye.

"Would now be a good time to talk about me keeping Greasle as a pet?"

Aunt Phil's eyes widened in surprise. She looked from

the two wyverns back to Greasle, then snorted. But it was with laughter, not temper. "You picked your moment well, there's no question."

"See, the thing is," Nate rushed to explain before she could say no, "you said that all these beasts were thought of as pests, back when there were so many of them. So maybe that could happen to gremlins, too. Maybe they're pests now, but they might not be forever?"

Aunt Phil's gaze sharpened as she put her hands on her hips. "Hoist by my own petard, eh?"

"I beg your pardon?"

"It means, I've been nicked by my own sword, my boy. Excellent argument."

Now it was Nate's turn to beam. He exchanged a hopeful glance with Greasle.

"However, this is a complicated request and we don't have much time to discuss it right now."

Nate's shoulders slumped, and he opened his mouth to argue, something he'd never dared to do before.

Aunt Phil held up a finger. "I'm not saying no, Nate. And I will admit, your gremlin has turned out to be more helpful than I ever could have imagined."

On his shoulder, Greasle swelled up with pride, just like a toad.

"All I'm saying is that time is running out on our deadline. We've still got to collect that wretch Obediah so we can tell Urien we've taken care of the problem. We've only got—" She glanced down at her watch. "Right. Could I have my watch back, please?"

"Oh, sure." Nate scrambled to unbuckle the strap and handed the watch to her.

She squinted at the time. "About an hour to spare," she said as she buckled it on. "Remind me we'll need to get you one of these."

"Yes, ma'am."

"Now, where was I?"

"We were to bring Obediah back to Urien."

"Right!" Aunt Phil turned to the wall where Obediah had been crouching in terror.

But the wall was empty.

Nate whipped his head around, but the other side of the cave was empty as well. "Where'd he go?"

"He's gone!" Aunt Phil said. "Along with my pack!"

Old Nudd rumbled something. Nate and Aunt Phil put

their ear trumpets in place, and Aunt Phil said, "Could you repeat that, please?"

"The slippery one left while Belli was hatching."

"We must go after him, then. Thank you, Nudd, for all your help. I hope you and little Belli enjoy each other's company."

The old wyvern turned his craggy head and looked directly at Nate. Old Nudd's eyes stilled, and Nate sucked in a breath. The old wyvern was letting him see into his soul. Showing him the contentment and gratitude he felt.

"You're welcome," Nate whispered.

Chapter Eighteen

A<small>S THEY WOUND THEIR WAY</small> up the tunnel that led from the treasury, Aunt Phil began talking to herself. "There are at least four different tunnels that man could have taken. How on earth will we find him?"

"He went this a-ways," Greasle said, pointing to the main tunnel.

"How do you know?" Aunt Phil asked.

The little gremlin shrugged. "I can smells him."

"Well." Aunt Phil was momentarily speechless. "That's

a helpful skill. Although you could have mentioned it earlier," she said dryly.

They quickened their pace, knowing there was a chance of finding him sooner rather than later. When the tunnel reached the main cavern, Aunt Phil held a finger to her lips. Nate nodded, then they peeked around the corner.

Obediah dangled from a rope halfway up the sheer cliff face. He swung Aunt Phil's pick into the rock and used it to hitch himself higher.

"Stop!" Aunt Phil said, stepping fully into view.

Obediah whipped his head around and sneered. "Or you'll what? Stop me? I don't think so." Then he unhooked the lantern hanging from his belt. "But just to be sure." He hurled the lantern toward them.

The glass shattered and the oil spilled out as the lantern hit the ground at their feet. With a faint whoosh, the kerosene burst into flames.

Aunt Phil shoved Nate back into the tunnel to avoid being burned. "If you ever return," she called to Obediah, "I'll let the wyverns have you. Consider yourself warned."

They both watched in helpless fury as Obediah made his way up the cliff. After a moment, Nate felt something run across his feet. He looked down to find a swarm of salamanders rushing toward the flames. They threw themselves into the fire, rolling around like pigs in mud. They glowed bright red and orange as their bodies absorbed the fire, putting it out.

"Did you know they could do that?" Nate asked.

"Yes, I just wish they could do it *faster*," Aunt Phil said.

By the time the salamanders put the flames out, Obediah had disappeared from sight. "He got away," Nate said, fearing that any hope they had of finding his parents had disappeared with him.

"Yes, he did," Aunt Phil said, her voice full of disappointment. "At least for now."

"Can't you do something?"

"Like what, Nate? He has all my climbing gear! And even if I managed to climb that cliff, he'd be gone before I reached him." Aunt Phil heaved a great sigh of frustration. "Well, at least the wyverns will calm down."

"I don't care about the stupid wyverns or the dumb Covenant," Nate said, clenching his fists. He wanted to pound them on the cave wall, he was so angry.

"Yes you do, Nate. You care very much. But you care for

your parents more, which is perfectly understandable."

Aunt Phil's being reasonable didn't make him feel any better.

"I'm not buying his explanation," she continued. "He's up to something, and he's shown us he can be quite ruthless in getting it."

"Does that mean you think my parents might be—"

"No, Nate. I'm sorry. Meeting Obediah hasn't changed my mind about that. Now come along. We'd best start making our way back so we can reach Urien before the deadline."

When they finally emerged from the wyverns' cavern, the daylight was beginning to fade. It grew even darker as a shadow moved overhead.

It was a wyvern. A giant one. Urien, Nate thought.

The dragon landed on the ground directly in front of Aunt Phil.

"Ear trumpets," she murmured.

Nate grabbed his and stuck it into his ear.

"You have removed the intruder," Urien said. "And just in time." He glanced over at the sun low on the horizon.

"And we've had a bit of luck with Old Nudd," Aunt Phil told the leader of the wyverns. "I think you'll find him a changed man—er, wyvern."

"Thank you," Urien said. "And once again, the Covenant stands." He glanced at Nate. "Would the two of you care for a ride back?"

"We would be honored, right, Nate?"

Unable to find his voice, Nate merely nodded. Honored, but terrified, too. How would they get up there? How would they stay on? "Best climb in the rucksack," he told Greasle.

"You don't have to tell me twice," she said.

Urien arced out one wing and laid the edge of it on the ground. Using the spines as a sort of ladder, Aunt Phil climbed up. Nate followed, surprised at how easy it was. The dragon's wing was smooth and strong, unlike anything he'd ever felt before.

Aunt Phil seated herself right where Urien's narrow neck

met his wings. Nate settled in behind her and held on for dear life. With a great leap, the wyvern launched himself into the air.

Nate's stomach fell so hard and fast, he thought he was going to be sick. But the wind rushing against his face quickly chased away the feeling. Screwing up his courage, he opened his eyes.

Far below, the ground spread out like thick green velvet. Bright blue lakes glittered jewel-like in the fading light. Except for the swish of Urien's great wings, everything was quiet. This was much, much better than an airplane, Nate thought.

All too soon, Urien reached Dewey's house. He circled once, then landed, a smooth, gliding finish that was much different from Aunt Phil's bouncy, jouncy landings. When he'd stopped, he swept one wing out toward the ground so they could climb off. Nate took his time, trying to memorize the feel of the dragon's skin under his hands.

When they were on the ground, Aunt Phil said, "Thank you for the ride."

Nate didn't have time to get his ear trumpet in place, but he was pretty sure the wyvern's rumble meant *You're*

welcome. Then Urien launched himself into the air and flew back to the mountains.

Nate had ridden a dragon. He could hardly wrap his mind around that. He had ridden a dragon and captured a basilisk and helped a phoenix egg hatch. Surely those things proved that anything was possible!

Anything.

Suddenly, it didn't matter if Aunt Phil believed his parents were still alive. *He* believed. He believed with all his heart. And he'd been right about a lot of things that Aunt Phil had been wrong about: trusting Greasle, *not* leaving his aunt in the wyverns' treasury, recognizing that the egg wasn't a dud.

Maybe he'd be right about this, too.

carrier pigeon: a specially trained pigeon who carries messages attached to its legs. An especially useful means of communication when traveling in the wilds where telegraphs and telephone wires do not reach.

coal: a black rock widely used as fuel.

Covenant: the binding agreement between wyverns and humans that severely limits the wyverns from rampaging or destroying humans and their property.

Dinas Emrys: the hillock where Lludd captured the wyverns and managed to bind them with the Covenant. Since then, it has become the traditional meeting place for parley talks between humans and wyverns.

ear trumpets: specially designed devices invented by Meridian Fludd in 1642. They were originally designed to amplify long-distance communications between ships, but were later adapted and modified by Llewellyn Fludd to re-shape and compress the sound waves made by wyverns so they are recognizable to the human ear.

geode: a rock that contains a cavity lined with crystals. Remarkably similar to wyvern egg duds.

The Geographica: the highly prized collection of Fludd maps of the world. There is only one in existence. Last seen being carried by Nathaniel's father, Horatio Fludd, before he was declared lost at sea.

gremlin: a small, oily creature about the size of a monkey with the face of a bat. Lurks primarily in engines and machinery. First discovered by World War I pilots.

juvies: wyverns who have reached two years of age. They sport all of the strength and skills of adult wyverns but none of their judgment or ability to reason.

Lludd: The heroic leader of Wales around 100 BC. With his brother's help, he managed to trap and ensnare the wyverns.

manticore: a rare and terrible beast with the body of a lion and the face of a man. Lives in the wilds of India. They are extremely hard to tame, and Gordon Fludd's companion is the only recorded instance of a manticore's being successfully kept in captivity.

mead: a honeyed drink that was instrumental in getting the wyverns to agree to the Covenant. Used today as a token offering to wyverns in parley protocol.

Muscovy: a medieval Russian area centered around Moscow.

Obediah Fludd: a direct descendant of Octavius Fludd. Carries the tradition of bitterness and intrafamily feud with the rest of the Fludd family.

Octavius Fludd: the black-sheep son of Mungo Fludd, who was given the northeast direction to explore. After years in the frozen wilds of Russia and Muscovy, he became bitter and paranoid.

parley: a formal attempt to meet and resolve a dispute.

regurgitating: when adult animals consume food, partially digest it, then bring it back up to feed their young.

salamanders: elemental creatures of fire. They are small, lizardlike beasts unharmed by flame.

Snowdonia: a forested area in Wales where the wyverns' territory is located.

treasury: one of the most carefully guarded areas of any dragons' cave where they keep the treasure they have accumulated throughout centuries of rampaging and collecting. Older dragons are often attracted to the warm glow thrown off by the treasure.

Wales: a country in the United Kingdom, to the west of England.

yearlings: wyverns who are one year of age or younger. Essentially harmless.

zeppelin: a rigid airship or dirigible.